WHEN THE NIGHT BIRD SINGS

A MECANA NOVELLA BY
JOHN L. LANSDALE

BOOKVOICE PUBLISHING 2018

When the Night Bird Sings Copyright © 2018
by John L. Lansdale
All rights reserved.

Design Copyright © 2018
by BookVoice Publishing
All rights reserved.

ISBN
978-0-9990361-2-9 Paperback
978-0-9990361-5-0 eBook

BookVoice Publishing
PO Box 1528
Chandler, TX 75758
www.bookvoicepublishing.com
www.bvpstore.com

THE MECANA SERIES by John L. Lansdale
#1 - Horse of a Different Color
#2 - When the Night Bird Sings
#3 - Twisted Justice
#4 – The Box

Titles by John L. Lansdale
Slow Bullet
Long Walk Home
Zombie Gold
The Last Good Day
Broken Moon
Shadows West (with Joe R. Lansdale)
Hell's Bounty (with Joe R. Lansdale)
Boy and Hog (Short Story)
Boy and Hog Return (Short Story)
Emergency Christmas (Short Story)
Tales from the Crypt (Comic Series)
That Hellbound Train (Graphic Novel)
Yours Truly, Jack the Ripper (Graphic Novel)
Shadow Warrior (Graphic Novel)
Justin Case (Graphic Novel)

Follow the author online at
www.bvpstore.com
www.bookvoicepublishing.com
www.twitter.com/mybookvoice
www.goodreads.com/johnllansdale
www.facebook.com/bookvoicepublishing

What Others are Saying about John L. Lansdale

"Mickey Spillane fans will welcome this page-turner... Lansdale effectively delays revealing the novel's big secret until the end. Those who like their thrillers with a heavy dose of violent action will be satisfied."
– *Publishers Weekly* review of **Slow Bullet**

"This is an entertaining, science fiction-historical-horror blend with resourceful protagonists and a solid cast of secondary characters." – *Booklist* review of **Zombie Gold**

"...the author's innate ability to spin a complex tale painted with vivid characters and intense suspense provides readers with a well-paced book that they may find difficult to set down...a worthwhile suspenseful ride."
– *Amazing Stories* review of **Horse of a Different Color**

"**Slow Bullet** is a straight-ahead thriller...it's about action, and there's plenty of that. Check it out."
– *Bill Crider's Pop Culture Magazine*

"**Zombie Gold** has something for everyone... It's exciting, entertaining and educational. A fun ride."
– Joan Hallmark, TV personality, actress and author

"...something unique and comfortable and difficult to put down. Highly recommended."
– *Cemetery Dance* review of **Hell's Bounty**

"True to Lansdale tradition, John L. Lansdale has compiled a piece of work that should appeal to a wide range of readers." – *Amazing Stories* review of **Zombie Gold**

For
Joe and Karen

"You do what's right because it's right. You don't have to have a reason."
Bud Lansdale

CHAPTER 1

I was standing inside my new office, admiring the freshly-painted sign on the open glass door, when she walked up and smiled.

"You open?"

"Yes ma'am," I said.

She had sparkling blue eyes and long, shiny blonde hair with red ruby earrings matching her sinuous lips. She was wearing a tight fire-red dress that showed all her dangerous curves. The big diamond on her left hand told me someone had staked a claim.

I invited her in with a gentlemanly gesture and closed the door. She walked in, stopped and tilted her head slightly and looked at me.

"You're Thomas Mecana, right?"

"Yes ma'am," I said.

"The one who solved The Mutilator case?"

"Along with my partner and a lot of others."

"I used to see Doctor Durant and Lisa at social functions from time to time but never met them."

"Lucky you."

"My name's Candy Kane," she said. "I saw the ad in the paper announcing your new private investigation business. I want to hire you, Mr. Mecana."

"Really," I said, contemplating her unusual name. "Have a seat, Mrs. Kane. Most people drop the mister and call me Mecana," I said. "You're our first client."

She sat down, crossed her long legs and looked at me.

I sat down in my new swivel chair behind the desk, but didn't cross my legs.

"I have a problem," she said. "It has to be kept hush-hush."

"I can be so quiet you could hear the proverbial pin drop."

"And what I tell you will be in confidence, right; it goes no further?" she said.

"Maybe my partner, that's it."

"Who's Connors?" she asked, pointing to the sign on the door.

"She was my partner on The Mutilator case. Darcie Connors, you can trust her. She will be here soon."

"How come you quit the police?"

"A long story," I said. "What can I do for you?"

"My husband and I need protection. I have reason to believe someone is trying to kill us."

"Why?"

"My husband is Ashton Kane, a psychotherapist M.D.," she began. "A stock broker he was treating has accused him of hypnotizing him and planting a plot in his mind to acquire a million dollars of his money. He filed a lawsuit three years ago against my husband but it was thrown out of court for lack of evidence. And now he's trying to kill us.

I think he shot a hole in the window of my car yesterday, missing my head by about two inches."

"What's his name?" I asked.

"Edward G. Fillmore. He's insane. I need someone to protect us."

"Your husband know about the window?"

"No. He's in New York to meet with Landon Fritz, a professor at the medical school Ashton attended where they became friends. I didn't want it to upset him."

"So you're whistling in the dark?" I said.

"What's that mean?" she asked.

"Means it could be anyone. Maybe an accident. Something my daddy used to say."

"It was no accident," she said.

"Then you should go to the cops."

"No cops, that's why I came to you."

"Could I see some ID please?"

"You don't believe me?"

"I don't trust myself."

She reached into a small purse she was holding and took out a Texas driver's license and laid it on the desk. The name she gave me was the one on the driver's license. I recognized her address as one in the upper crust sections of suburbia Dallas. And she was 28, still in the youthful splendor phase of life.

"Thank you," I said.

She picked the license up and put it back in her purse.

"I'm willing to pay you a hundred thousand dollars to silence this nut in whatever way you see fit as long as it's permanent and soon. Do we have a deal?" She held out her hand.

"You've got the wrong man. You're looking for a hit-man, not a private investigator."

"I'll double that," she said. "Two hundred thousand."

"Not even for that."

"Very well," she said. "I'm sure someone will see it my way."

She stood up and I did too. She reached for the pen my daughter Emily had given me and wrote down a phone number. She shoved the notepad toward me.

"If you change your mind call me."

"Tempting, but no cigar," I said.

"You talk in riddles, Mecana."

"It's my daddy's fault."

She looked even more perplexed. "Think about it. Half up front," she said.

"You know I have to call the cops?" I said.

"For what? I thought our discussion was in confidence."

"It was, until you got around to discussing murder," I said.

"I don't know what you're talking about," she said. "I was asking you to persuade him to leave us alone."

"That's not what I heard," I said.

She laid the pen back on my desk and walked to the door and opened it. She stopped in the open doorway and looked at me over her shoulder. "There could be other re-wards," she said and ran her tongue over her bright red lips.

"Some days are harder than others to navigate," I said. "I think this is one of them."

"Your daddy?" she asked.

"Nope, me," I said.

She smiled again and walked out, leaving the door open.

I stood at the open door and watched her hips sway back and forth as her red high heels clicked on the shiny tile floor to the elevator. It was a tempting sight.

I closed the door and sat back down at my desk, picked up Emily's pen and looked at the phone number she wrote down on the pad. A voice in my head that sounded like my daddy said, "Don't even think about it." I wadded the paper up and threw it in the trash can.

About ten minutes after Mrs. Kane left, Darcie showed up with two sacks of paper, folders, pens and other office supplies, looking beautiful as usual with a black dress to match her short black hair and dark brown eyes.

I usually didn't wear a suit but I was glad I did today. Jeans and a pullover would have clashed with her little black dress ensemble she had on for our first day.

She sat the sacks on her new desk. "Where's the coffee?" she said, looking at an empty coffee pot on a table next to the wall.

"I've been busy," I said. "I can make some."

"No, I'm good," she said. "You left early this morning. I'm no Sara Lee but I would have fixed you breakfast if you had waited."

"That would have been nice but I had to be here to unlock the office for the painter so we would be ready for our first day. What do you think?" I said, pointing at the door.

"Alright, except I think it would have had a better ring to it if it was 'Connors and Mecana Private Investigators.'"

"Never thought about it."

"I know. Men don't like women on top unless it's their idea."

"I'll have them change the damn thing."

"Forget it, its fine," she said.

"Then why are we talking about it?"

"I smell perfume," she said, changing the subject.

"A Mrs. Candy Kane was here."

"You're kidding," she said.

"No, that's her name. She had the driver's license to prove it. She thinks a former psych patient of her husband is trying to murder them. She wants me to snuff him before he does the same to her."

"She give you a name?" Darcie asked.

"A stock broker named Edward G. Fillmore who thinks Mr. Kane hypnotized him out of a million dollars."

"Gets right to it, doesn't she?" Darcie said.

"She offered me a hundred thousand and when I refused it she raised the price to two hundred thousand. Her husband doesn't know about the offer."

"He's better off not knowing, he would be an accomplice," Darcie said. "You know her?"

"Never saw her before. She said she saw our ad in the paper."

"You know she will find someone that will probably do it for less. You going to make the call, or do I?"

"I'll do it," I said. "Verves will be surprised to hear from me so soon. I told her our conversation was in confidence but that was before we got around to discussing murder."

"You record the conversation?"

"I forgot the recorder. She left her phone number but I threw it in the trash."

"Verves might want it," she said.

"Yeah." I reached in the trash can and picked up the paper with Kane's number on it. "You sure you're alright with the sign?" I said.

"Yes its fine," she said, smiled and batted her big brown eyes.

Beautiful women know they have a hypnotic effect over a man whatever their profession is while working their charms to get whatever it is they want. She knew damn well I'd have the sign changed because I don't want to sleep alone for however long the punishment is for a crime I didn't know I committed until I was verbally convicted.

She sat down at her desk and looked around the office. "This place looks a little drab. I think I'll get some pictures for the walls, and maybe a plant or two."

"Fine with me," I said and propped my feet up on my desk and gazed out the sixth floor window at the interstate. The morning traffic had slowed to a trickle before lunch time. I couldn't get Mrs. Kane off my mind.

"First rule, no feet on the desk," Darcie said.

"That's my thinking position," I said.

"Find another one," she said.

I dropped my feet back on the floor. "I don't think it's going to work, I've been doing it too long."

"You'll get over it. Maybe we should put a partition between the desks to create an illusion of privacy when we're talking to clients."

"Whatever," I said.

"You going to call Verves?" she said.

"Yes." I fished my phone out of my pocket and dialed his number.

Robert Verves was a small black man who used his intuition, intelligence and Hercules-like strength to rise from recruit to Navy SEAL to Chief of Homicide in record time.

"Hello, Mecana. The new name is showing up on Caller ID," he said.

"Darcie and I opened our PI office today."

"What about her twin, is she in with you?"

"No, she decided she would rather face the dangers of teaching."

"Good for her. I received some forms a while back the state sent me to verify your employment for your PI licenses. I gave you good marks."

"Thanks," I said. "I had a visit from a pretty lady this morning before the paint could dry on my door, asking me to cancel a guy. I think she was serious. Thought you should know."

"What do you have on her?" Verves asked.

"Her name is Candy Kane, believe it or not. Kane with a 'K.' I verified it with her driver's license. The address on her license was a penthouse at the Ellison Plaza hotel."

"The uptown crowd," Verves said.

"Yep."

"Who's her intended victim?" Verves asked.

"Edward G. Fillmore," I said. "Fillmore is a stock broker and a former patient of Dr. Ashton Kane, Mrs. Kane's husband. Dr. Kane is a psychotherapist - hypnotizes his patients - he's in New York now."

"What was Fillmore's problem," Verves said.

"She said he was insane."

"Not very descriptive," Verves said.

"He sued the doctor for hypnotizing him to get his money but it was thrown out for lack of evidence. She said someone shot a hole in the driver's window of her car yesterday, just missing her, and she thinks it was Fillmore. I haven't seen the car."

"I'll put somebody on it and let you know," Verves said.

"Good, when I told her I would have to call the police she tried to change her story.

She's in a hurry so you should be, too. I got her phone number."

"Give it to me," Verves said. "Seems like I've heard that story before but we couldn't find any proof on the doctor. I'll check it out again."

As I talked to Verves I watched Darcie bend over her desk using her arms as measuring sticks for the length of her desk, weird fantasies ran through my warped brain.

"You can have your old job back anytime you want," he said.

"Thanks but I'll try this for a while. Talk to you later," I said and hung up.

"Is he going to get on it?" Darcie asked.

"Yes, he said he'll get back to me."

"I'm going to look for some picture and plants," she said. "You want to meet me at Brogans for lunch? I know men don't like shopping for anything that doesn't fire bullets or have an engine so I won't ask you to go with me."

"That's very considerate of you. I'll find something to keep me busy until lunch."

"Okay, see you at noon." She opened the door and looked at the sign for a long moment, stepped outside, closed the door and was gone.

I looked around the office at the blank white walls and the slow turning white ceiling fans with little designer bulbs in the light fixtures. Darcie was right, it did need something but it wasn't changing the sign.

I took off my tie and propped my feet back on the desk. What she doesn't know won't hurt me. I picked up the pen Emily gave me and thought about the promises I made to my two daughters that I couldn't afford to keep. A new convertible for Emily's high school graduation was going to cost thirty thousand dollars and Morgan's trip to Disneyland for graduating to high school was probably another five thousand, with no idea where the money was coming from unless I drained my savings.

My ex sure wasn't going to help. She said it was my promises and my problem.

Maybe I would have to kill someone.

Taking Darcie's comment to heart, I decided to go kick some tires on a new truck to pass the time until lunch. I wasn't sure I wanted another truck. Even if I had the money to buy one, the one I had was like an old friend I would hate to say goodbye to.

I would never tell anyone that because they would think I was kind of weird and I already had too many weird things going for me.

The weirdest one was the box I took to the crime locker evidence room from The Mutilator case. If anyone ever opened that up I might be in more trouble than I could handle.

Chapter 2

It had been a while since I was at Brogans Restaurant. It wasn't fancy but it was clean and the food was good. It was where most of the locals went for lunch or dinner when they wanted to take a step up from a fast food place. They had a semi-maître d' who watched you come in and said hello but let you seat yourself.

Darcie was sitting in a booth sipping red wine when I got there. I sat down, she smiled and pointed at her wine glass.

"No, I think I'll have a salad," I said. "I haven't been to the gym this week and I feel it."

"I'll have a salad, too," she said. "Want to go to the gym after work today?"

"That would be now. We don't have any work," I said.

"Well you could have made two hundred thousand if you didn't have a conscience," Darcie said.

"Yeah, I know, but mostly I didn't want a boyfriend named Bubba. Let's see if we can snag a waiter."

"You're going to be surprised," she said.

"About what?" I asked.

"You'll see," she said.

I looked up and it took me a minute to realize it was DeMax Baker walking to the table. DeMax was wearing black pants, a white shirt with a name tag and a bowtie. He had cut his bushy hair short and put on weight. He didn't look much like I remembered.

"Mecana. What it is?"

"Man, do you look different," I said.

"Only on the outside," he said, and smiled.

"What are you doing here?"

"I'm a working man now. A bonifide server."

"You look the part," I said.

"Yep, what can I get you?"

"Okay, Mr. Server, could we have two house salads with ranch, and I'll have a Coke," I said.

"I got it," DeMax said and wrote in his pad. "Would you like more wine, Miss Darcie?"

"No, I'm good, DeMax," she said.

"That's two house salads with ranch dressing and a Coke for Mecana, right?"

"Right," I said.

"Coming up," he said, stuck his notepad in his pocket and walked away.

"You're right," I said. "I am surprised. DeMax and work don't seem to fit in the same sentence."

"Looks like he's changed his ways," Darcie said.

"I don't know, I think I'll wait a while to pass judgment. DeMax is pretty shrewd.

He may be working an angle of some kind here. If he is I would bet a woman is involved."

"You are a Doubting Thomas aren't you," Darcie said.

"Oh...That was cute," I said.

"I thought so," she said, smiled and took a sip of wine.

"You find some stuff for the office?" I asked.

"Yes, I'll drop if off at the office after lunch and meet you at the gym," she said. "You think that sweet-smelling Candy lady will drop in again?"

"I don't think so."

"She might not, but she may send someone. I don't think it would be a social call. Some people can't handle rejection"

"I'll make a note of that, partner," I said.

DeMax came back to the table carrying a tray. "Here you are," he said. He placed the salads and Coke on the table, picked up the tray and looked at Darcie. "Miss Darcie, thanks again for getting me out of that mess with the police. You sure are a good lawyer."

"You're welcome, DeMax. They needed a suspect and were willing to do whatever they could to get one, including railroading an innocent man."

"I sure was that. I wouldn't kill all those pretty ladies."

"With your fondness for women," I said, "we had already come to that conclusion."

"Hope I didn't have anything to do with ya'll quitting the police," DeMax said.

"You didn't, it was mostly politics," Darcie said.

"We just didn't fit there anymore," I said. "We opened a Private Investigation office," I said, handing him a business card.

"That's what Miss Darcie said. You need anything, all you have to do is ask. I owe you," he said and stuck the card in his pocket.

23

"You don't owe us anything, DeMax," Darcie said. "The legal system owes you."

"Well, just the same. If you need me you know where I am," he said.

"We'll remember that," I said.

DeMax nodded and walked away.

"How long you think he'll be here?" Darcie asked.

"Good question," I said. "DeMax marches to his own drum."

"I think I'll go," she said. "I'll see you at the gym."

"You barely touched your salad," I said.

"I'm not very hungry," she said, finished off the wine and stood up. "Watch your back. I have a bad feeling about Candy Kane."

"I'll be okay. See you at the gym," I said.

"You can get the check," she smiled. "And give DeMax a big tip."

CHAPTER 3

The lunch crowd was leaving the gym when I pulled in. I saw Darcie's SUV and parked my Silverado beside it. When I went in I saw Darcie's trainer Mindy showing an overweight young lady how to use a treadmill. Two gym rats were lifting weights.

Mindy saw me, we waved at each other.

When I came out of the locker room in my gym shorts and Marine t-shirt Mindy was talking to Darcie. As I walked up to them she smiled.

"Hi Mecana haven't seen you for a while," she said.

"I know, been busy getting our office open."

"Anything I can get you?" she asked.

"No, I think I'm good."

"Okay, have a good workout. I've got a class to teach. See you."

"Yeah, see you," I said as she walked away. I turned to Darcie. "What were you two talking about?"

"You," Darcie said. "About what a good-looking dude you are with those sexy gray eyes and that bod. I think she wants to play nice-nice with you."

"What do you think about that?" I said and grinned.

"Fine, I'll go home and pack since it's your house," she said.

"Not to worry. Not my type."

"Then I won't pack. For now."

"Good. I would be lonesome."

"Not for long if she knew I was gone."

"I don't know, I suspect she may have more interest in you."

"Not into that sort of thing. I have enough trouble with you."

"You know the house can be yours, too. We can go to a Justice of the Peace or do the whole ball of wax wedding thing."

"That's a subject for another day," she said, pushed the treadmill button and started running.

After a good two-hour workout I had had enough. "Think I'll call it good and take a shower. Want to take one with me?" I said.

"I think management frowns on coed showering," she said.

"Party poopers," I said.

"That doesn't mean we can't take another one when we get home," she said, and
winked.

"Time to go," I said, picked up my towel and headed for the locker room.

We stopped by the office to look at the new things Darcie bought. The place looked a lot more alive with reprints of dead painters' art on the walls and a couple of artificial plants. She even got us nameplates to set on our desk.

"It's looks great," I said. "Can we go now?"

"What's your hurry," she said.

"We were going to take a shower together?"

"Maybe," she said and stopped at the door, looked at the sign again and sighed.

"I'll take care of it," I said, locked the door and headed home.

I got a call from Chief Verves two days later.

"Mecana, they found Mr. Kane dead this morning in a New York City hotel with four 9mm slugs in him, all in his heart," Verves said. "I got someone on the way to see Mrs. Kane. His buddy Landon Fritz said he had dinner with him at the hotel and went home around ten that night."

"Fritz have any family?" I asked.

"Said he didn't but we're still checking him out," Verves said.

"She wasn't whistling Dixie," I said. "Sounds like the hitman beat her to the punch."

"Yeah, I'll let you know," he said and hung up.

Darcie walked in the room with a towel wrapped around her head and another around her body. "Who was that?" she asked.

"Verves. They found Candy's husband full of holes in a New York hotel very dead.

Maybe I should have been more sympathetic about her situation before I turned her away."

"You did the right thing," she said. "But she may not think so."

"Why didn't you wait for me?" I said. "I kinda liked the coed showering the other day."

"Go take a cold shower by yourself," she said.

"Won't change anything," I said.

"Well switch gears, we've got an insurance company man coming. He has some work for us."

"Do you know you're naked?"

"Knock it off and get ready," she threw the towel wrapped around her waist at me and walked back to the bedroom buck naked.

CHAPTER 4

We arrived at the office at ten the next morning. Darcie made coffee and a Mister Summers from the insurance company showed up a short time later. He was middle-aged, trim with thin gray hair and glasses, wearing a light gray suit and a red tie.

"Congratulations on your new business," he said. "I saw your ad."

"Looks like that ad was money well spent," I said. "Have a seat, Mr. Summers."

He sat down and placed his briefcase beside the chair.

"Would you like some coffee?" Darcie asked.

"No thank you," he picked up his briefcase, opened it and took some papers out. He looked at Darcie like he was inhaling her, placed the papers on my desk and sat the briefcase back beside the chair.

"I think we have some claim adjusters taking kickbacks. That's the information you will need to check out," he said, motioning toward the papers on my desk. "We had a client tell us he paid off one of our claim adjusters to get the figure he wanted. There may be more. We don't want to handle this in-house, they might catch on."

I picked up the papers, took a quick look, nodded and handed them to Darcie.

She looked at them and leaned against my desk facing the man. "Mr. Summers, this may take a day or it may take a month, depending on what we have to do. We charge five hundred a day plus expenses. You only pay for the days we are working on your case."

"That will be fine. Let me know when you finish your investigation," he said.

I thought it would be. She could have sold him the Brooklyn Bridge.

"The first five hundred is up front, Mr. Summers," I said. "We'll bill you for the rest."

"I came prepared," he said. "I have a signed check. I'll fill it out."

"Make it out to Conner's and Mecana Private Investigators," I said, looked at Darcie and grinned. She didn't show any expression, I didn't think she heard me. He made out the check and handed it to me, picked up his briefcase and stood up.

"Thank you," I said and shook his hand.

"We'll keep in touch with you, Mr. Summers," Darcie said.

"Thank you," he said and walked to the door. I opened it and he walked out.

I held the check up and looked at it before handing it to Darcie. "Our first money," I said. "You want to make the deposit?"

"I can't until you change the name at the bank to Conner's and Mecana."

"You did hear me," I said. "It was a joke, you're trying to rattle my cage."

"I don't think they will take it," she said.

"Quit rubbing it in and take the check to the bank," I said. "I'll see if I can come up with some information on the claims adjuster."

"Alright, we'll see," she waved the check at me and left.

I stared at the sign on the door and poured myself a cup of Darcie's coffee and sat back down at my desk, propped my feet up and took a sip. It felt like my eyes were going to cross. It was worse than the stuff Verves made at the station. I was glad she didn't give it to Mr. Summers or we might not have a client.

I was still gagging when my phone rang. It was Candy Kane.

"Mecana, Ashton is dead," she said.

"I heard, I'm very sorry. Have you talked to the police?"

"A cop showed up to tell me about Ashton, asked some questions and left."

"Why did you call me?" I said.

"I need your protection," she said.

"Not interested," I said.

"Mecana you're the only one I can turn to."

"We've already discussed your situation; the cops are your best bet."

"You don't have to do anything you don't want to," she said. "Just keep me alive. Someone took another shot at me when I pulled into the hotel parking lot last night. Just missed me, it went over my head as I got out of the car."

"Where had you been?" I said.

"Shopping. I was lonesome, please."

I knew it wasn't a good idea but the please part got to me. "Did the bullet hit anything? A post, a trash can, anything?"

"Not that I know of," she said.

"We can talk but I'm not promising anything," I said.

"There's a 'K' on the door, top floor of the Ellison hotel," she said and was gone.

I considered calling Verves, but decided to hear her out first. I stuck the insurance folder in my desk and dumped the bad coffee in the trash can.

On my way to the hotel, I called Darcie and told her to meet me to check out this Candy lady.

"Wait for me before you go up," Darcie said.

"Meet you in the lobby," I said. I wasn't sure if she was conscientious, cautious, jealous or all three.

I had just walked in the hotel when Darcie showed up.

"You deposit the check?" I said.

"They took it with some reluctance," she said and smiled.

"Never give up do you?"

"Nope. What have we got here?"

"I told her we would talk," I said. "I didn't make any promises."

"You go on up. I'll make sure no one is following you," Darcie said.

"Okay, it's a penthouse on the top floor, room K." I got on the elevator alone while Darcie waited for the next one.

I got off on the top floor and walked down a long hall with Ansel Adams photographs hanging on the walls. I rang the buzzer and stood to one side of the door with the "K" on it, waiting.

A voice from the other side asked, "Who is it?"

"Mecana," I said and she opened the door. I walked in and she closed it quickly.

"Am I glad to see you," she said.

"You should let the cops handle this," I said.

"I was afraid they would arrest me."

"Should they? Did you have anything to do with your husband's murder?"

"Of course not. How could I? I was in Dallas."

I looked around the massive room. I always thought of motels and hotels as a place for two things, and the only thing that was required for both was a bed and privacy. This place had large windows with a view of jets taking off and landing at DFW. Wall-to-wall folding doors stood at one end of the room, opening to a bedroom where I could see a king-sized bed that had not been slept in for several days.

The doorbell rang.

"Oh no," she said, and gasped.

"I think that's my partner Darcie, she was covering my back." I walked over and stood beside the door. "Darcie?"

"Yes," she said. I unlocked the door and let her in.

"This is Mrs. Candy Kane, Darcie."

Darcie acknowledged her by looking her up and down. "You want a private investigator or a hitman, Mrs. Kane?"

"I need you to find a hitman before he finds me."

"Your husband have any family?" I said.

"Ashton's parents were killed in a plane crash when he was ten. He grew up in his aunt's home. She helped pay his way through medical school. He doesn't have any siblings, kids or ex-wives that I'm aware of."

"What about the sister? Where is she now?" I asked.

"She died last year from cancer," Candy said.

"Anyone else?" I said.

"Not that I know of."

"The cops won't cost you anything," I said. "But we will."

"No cops," she reiterated. "I don't want our lives plastered all over the news."

"You may not have a choice," Darcie said. "We'll have to call the cops and let them know we're working for you. If we decide to."

"Then you'll do it?" she asked.

I looked at Darcie and she nodded yes.

"As long as you understand that we're getting paid to solve the case. The two hundred thousand you offered, plus five hundred a day for expenses - with half the fee in cash now," I said.

I checked Darcie's reaction to my proposal and she nodded her head.

"Okay with me," Candy said.

Darcie and I looked at each other surprised. She went for the deal.

"We've got to get you to a safer place," I said.

"I'll pack some things," she said. "I have to handle Ashton's funeral when they ship his body back to Dallas."

"We'll help you take care of it. Where's your car?" I said.

"In my parking spot in the parking garage. Same as my age, 28."

"We'll leave it there. Give me the keys," I said. "I'll check for a bullet in the parking lot."

"Can't that wait? I'm afraid. I want to get out of here."

She did look very frightened. "Okay, I'll come back later."

"Darcie, why don't you get us a rental and I'll have a talk with Novel and let you know

where we're going to stay. May be someone on our trail already."

"Could be, call me," Darcie said and walked out.

"Where are we going?" Candy asked.

"I have to make a call to a friend of mine and find us a safe place at one of his real estate listings."

"That's kind of odd," she said.

"It works," I said. "Done it before."

"What's your daddy do?" she asked.

"Retired Marine Colonel. Unfortunately, he's dead."

"I'm sorry to hear that." After a short pause she changed the subject. "Are you as good as they say you are, Mecana?"

"Depends on what you mean," I said.

"Whatever I want it to be," she said and smiled.

"Maybe," I said.

"You better be."

CHAPTER 5

I called my fat friend Novel who said he had a place on Lake Tawakoni that would be available for a month. The occupants were on vacation in France. He gave me the code for the front gate. We both knew we weren't supposed to do it but we did. He said there was a key in the fork of a tree on the front lawn and he would pick up a sneaky five-thousand-dollar check for a month tomorrow. I told him to give me an address and I would mail it to him. We were on a case where visitors weren't welcome. He said he would do that if I would feed the fish, so I agreed.

I drove to the lake with Candy. The place was for high-rollers judging by the size of it. Candy should feel right at home. I drove on by, looking for a tail but didn't see one; made the block and waited for fifteen minutes before going into the lake property.

"What're you doing?" Candy asked.

"Checking for a tail, we'll use the car Darcie is picking up when we go out again," I said. Took one last look – still no traffic – drove up to the gate, punched the code and we drove through the drive and down to a large bungalow on the waterfront.

I grabbed her bags, found the key in the tree, and we made our way to the back of the house. Out on the lake, sailboats were whizzing along in a strong breeze while ski boats were pulling happy skiers. A bunch of white ducks saw us on the lawn and hurried to us. When they realized we didn't have anything to give them they waddled away.

When I turned the key a dark, tinted glass door disappeared into the wall and we walked in the room. Inside there was a large round bed, a Jacuzzi tub, multi-colored lights built into the walls and an electric star light ceiling with a white bear skin rug lying on the thick carpet by the bed.

"If it's alright with you," I said, "I don't want you in a bedroom that leads outside. Let's find another one."

"Okay with me. I have to take a bath, if you hear me scream come running," she said.

"You'll think it's Superman," I said.

We walked down a hall and came to a bedroom bigger than my den and I put her suitcases on the bed. "Don't let anyone know where you are and don't order food."

"I'm not going to like this," she said.

"I'm not either, but if someone is out to kill you…"

"There is," she said. "I'm going to take a bath."

I nodded and walked back out to the massive living room, sat on a twenty-foot-long white couch and looked at a wall-to-wall stone fireplace.

A large aquarium was built into another wall. Bigger fish than I've ever caught were swimming around in it. I got up and walked over to the aquarium and picked up the fish food and shook a large amount into the tank. A feeding frenzy began. I went back to the couch and called Darcie.

"I think I can find it," she said. "Where's Candy?"

"Taking a bath."

"No coed bathing Mecana," she said.

"Of course not," I said.

"I'm going to buy some TV dinners, we may have to eat in for a while. I rented a blue van," she said.

"Good." I hung up and called Verves.

"Mecana?" he said. "Are you in trouble?"

"Candy Kane is with me," I said.

"That's a surprise," he said. "Figured you'd pissed her off."

"May have but she's hired us. I promised her you wouldn't arrest her when I called you. Did I lie?"

"No, I don't have any evidence to arrest her. I checked out the stock broker Fillmore, he was in London when Mr. Kane was murdered. He said Candy was an evil woman. We woke Mrs. Kane up this morning to tell her. New York gave the investigation back to us.

I would like to talk to Mrs. Kane, for the record. We didn't find anything that would have put her in New York when her husband was murdered."

"She would have had to make a round-trip flight in one night. Possible, but not probable," I said.

"Time of death was early this morning according to New York. Think I agree with you for now, but I still have to talk to her."

"I'm keeping her under wraps for now while I find out who the players are. Have someone meet me at Bleaker's Bowling Alley on 34th at three this afternoon."

"I'll send Benny Modele," he said.

"Is that the guy who always dresses to the hilt and looks like he lost his best friend?"

"Yeah, that's him."

"Have him come alone. No one else. Do I have your word?"

"You got it," he said.

"Tell him he may not see me when he comes in but I'll see him."

"What little we know so far looks like it was a professional hit. The only fingerprints in the room were Kane's," Verves said.

"That's what I was thinking. Three o'clock at the bowling alley," I said again and hung up.

"How long do we have to stay here," Candy asked as she walked in the room.

"I don't know," I said. "Maybe until we find the killer."

"I made plans to move to France after I bury Ashton," she said.

"Did you make those plans before or after he was murdered?"

"After," she said. "Keep me alive until I leave and I'll pay you."

"If that's what you want," I said.

"I heard you talking to someone," she said.

"The cops. We have to meet a detective this afternoon. They want to ask you some questions. You don't have to go to the police station. I arranged for it to be on our terms."

"No, I won't go."

"They just want to talk to you. There's nothing to worry about."

"No," she flatly said.

"I give you my word. That's it. They're not going to arrest you. Why are you so worried?"

"I don't trust them. I don't want the cops to put me through hell for nothing."

"I'm not sure I trust them, either, but I do trust my former boss. He's always been true to his word."

"He better be or I won't trust you anymore," she said and disappeared back in the bathroom.

I sat down and waited.

CHAPTER 6

Darcie showed up at the house about an hour later with a stack of frozen TV dinners.

Darcie and I ate chicken but Candy almost threw up looking at hers. Funny how money can change your appetite. She refused to eat so we headed for the bowling alley.

We pulled up to a restaurant across the street from the bowling alley about five minutes early.

"I'm not eating here, either," Candy said.

"We not going here, it's the bowling alley across the street. I'll go check it out. Darcie, drive around the block. Anyone shows up who shouldn't, haul ass."

I got out on the passenger side between the car and the restaurant and hurried inside the restaurant. Darcie drove away with Candy while I cased the bowling alley from the restaurant. It usually wasn't hard to spot an unmarked police car. They drove solid white or black big-engine Ford or Dodges most of the time.

A black Challenger drove up in front of the bowling alley and Detective Bennie Modele got out of the car and went inside alone. I watched for about ten minutes for another car to show up but it didn't. I called Darcie and told her to pull into the alleyway beside the bowling alley.

The owner Henry usually left the back door unlocked during working hours so his employees could come and go from the back when they took smoking breaks. I hung out here when I was a kid and even did some pin work before they were automated.

Henry Bleaker had owned Bleaker's Bowling Alley since he came back from the Korean War with a chest full of medals, a Korean wife and a gimpy leg. He never had any kids, said he didn't think he would be a good father, but he was always good to me.

He was past eighty now, and slumped over when he walked. His hair was white and thin and his face showed the marks of time, but he showed up for work every day, rain or shine.

About a year ago I had stopped in to see how he was doing. The place looked a step away from the wrecking ball and was mostly a watering hole for the wrong kind of people these days. Addicts shooting up in the bathrooms, whores working the bar and the street outside. I knew he didn't have any other place to go so I put in a word for him with the street cops to cut him some slack.

I crossed the street and walked in the front door. Modele was standing at the end of the bar with a beer. An old man was trying to bowl but could barely lift the bowling ball. Two painted-up young women with very little on were sitting at the bar, drinking what looked like water. I saw one of them nudge the other and they looked my way.

I gave them a look back, shook my head no and the message was delivered.

Henry was sitting behind the bar working his obsolete cash register as usual.

He saw me and smiled as I walked up to the bar. "Tommy," he said. "Where in the hell have you been? I haven't seen you for ages."

"Playing cop, Henry, how're you doing?"

"Still here, want a beer?"

"Maybe later, got a little business to conduct with that fellow at the end of the bar," I said.

"Man has to take care of his business. Good to see you, Tommy."

"You too," I said. He was the only one in the world that called me Tommy.

Modele looked up, sat his beer down and walked over to me.

"You Mecana?" he asked.

"Yeah. Modele?"

"Yes, knew you by your reputation. Don't mention the beer to anyone, okay?" he said. "I normally don't drink unless I want to look like someone else."

I wasn't sure what that meant and didn't want to find out.

Bennie Modele was in his forties, a confirmed bachelor, over six-feet-tall, with short black hair and brown eyes. He spent a lot of money on clothes and looked more like a banker than a cop. The lines on his forehead showed most of the time and the corners of his mouth drooped slightly at the edges like he was always expecting his worse day ever.

"She here?" he asked, his dead-pan expression never changing.

"She's here," I said.

"Let's get this over with," he said. "I've got other appointments."

"Follow me," I said and headed for the back of the bowling alley.

As we stepped out the backdoor, a black Mercedes turned into the alley and rammed the back of our rental, slamming it into a dumpster. A big man dressed in black jumped out of the passenger seat carrying an AK-47. He took aim at Candy through the back glass.

Darcie saw him in the rearview mirror, pushed Candy to the floor, opened the driver's door and rolled out under the car with her Beretta in hand.

I grabbed the shooter from behind and we fell to the ground, wrestling for the gun. Out of the corner of my eye I saw the driver make his exit from the car, wearing the same type of clothing as the other man, and firing an Uzi at Modele. Several bullets from the Uzi hit Modele in the arm and leg and he fell to the ground, blood spilling out of his tailor-made gray suit. Everything was happening at microsecond speed.

Darcie rolled out from under the car and emptied her Beretta into the driver. He fell down beside Modele, their blood running together as it traveled across the dirty concrete alley.

I was hanging on the AK-47, trying to pull it from the shooter's grasp while Darcie was scrambling to reload. He jerked free and stood up. I drew my Glock and put three bullets in his head as fast as I could pull the trigger. He fell forward, bounced off the car, dropped his gun and collapsed to the concrete in a puddle of blood.

Darcie had the Beretta reloaded with no one to shoot.

I bent down and checked the pulse of the men. The shooters were both dead. Modele was unconscious but alive. He was having that worse day ever.

Henry and three other people were peeking out the open backdoor. When they realized the shooting had stopped they ventured out to take a closer look.

"I called 911, Tommy," Henry said.

"Thanks, Henry."

Darcie holstered her Beretta, walked over to Modele and kneeled down beside him. The arm was just grazed but blood was pouring out of his leg. She unbuckled Modele's belt and pulled it free of his pants, ejected the clip from his pistol, extracted the round in the chamber and wrapped the belt around his leg, ran it through the trigger guard and twisted it into a tourniquet and tied it to his leg with his red silk necktie.

We could hear the sounds of the sirens getting closer.

I walked over to the bullet-riddled car and looked at Candy. She was crouched down in the front floorboard in a fetal position, her hands covering her head.

"Are you hit," I asked.

"No," she said. "Did you kill them?"

"Yes. I need you to take a look, see if you know them."

"No, get me outta here," she said.

"Get out of the car," I said.

She slowly slid back up on the seat and looked at me. I opened what remained of the door. She got out of the car, slipped off her high heels, held them in her hand and walked over to the dead men.

"I don't know them," she said, cringing at their bodies.

"Would your husband have known them?"

"I don't think so," she said.

"Henry, you still got that restored '58 pickup?"

"I do," he said.

"Can I borrow it?" I asked.

"Sure, Tommy," he said. "I don't need it anyway, my licenses has expired." He fished the keys out of his pocket and handed them to me.

"You know how to drive a stick shift, Darcie?" I said.

"Better than you. What do you want to do?"

"Take Candy back to the lake. I'll take a taxi when I think it's safe to go, if I don't wind up in jail."

"I think we just stepped in a world of shit, Mecana," Darcie said.

"Yeah, we're going to earn that money," I said.

"The cops aren't going to like us leaving."

"We have to find out what the truth is but we can't do that if Candy's in the slammer."

"Okay," she said, holding out her hand for the keys. "I see the truck."

"Candy, go with Darcie, she's going to get you out of here."

"Thank goodness," she said and followed Darcie to the truck, still holding her shoes in her hand. I followed behind them.

The engine started and Darcie looked at me. "I'm glad it wasn't your truck that got shot up. I would hate to see a grown man cry."

"Me too," I said. "You buy insurance on the car?"

"Of course," she said.

"We're going to need it," I said.

Darcie smiled and drove away.

I checked Modele. The tourniquet was holding. He was unconscious but alive. The two hitmen didn't have a wallet or any papers on them. Before I could check the Mercedes, a police cruiser came to a squeaking halt in the alley. Two uniformed cops got out, weapons drawn. I knew one of them.

"Sergeant Nelson," I said. "I thought you retired?"

He shook his head no. "I didn't expect to see you here, Mecana. You go back to work?"

"No, working as a private eye now."

"Is Modele alive?" he asked.

"For now," I said.

"What happened here?"

"The two dead ones tried to blow us away."

"They must not have known who they were messing with," he grinned and holstered his weapon. The younger cop did the same.

"They weren't rabbit hunting, not with those guns," Nelson said.

Sergeant Nelson was a small man with big brown puppy-dog-eyes, a beer belly and a whiskey nose.

"This is my partner, Officer Sid Gilliam," Nelson said. "I'm teaching him the ropes until I retire."

Sid was an athletic-looking young man with bright blue eyes and blonde hair. He looked like he was born about the time Nelson became a cop.

He stuck out his hand. "I've heard of you, Mecana, you're one of the best. Nice to meet you," he said as we shook hands.

"Thanks," I said. "I don't feel very competent right now, almost got my client killed."

An ambulance made a quick turn into the alley with the deafening sound of the siren shaking the walls. The ambulance stopped, the siren stopped and two well-built paramedics jumped out with a gurney.

"Any of them alive?" one of the medics yelled, to anyone listening.

"Detective Modele, the one with the tourniquet on his leg," I said.

One medic hurried to him and checked his vitals, inserted an IV into Modele's arm, strapped him on the gurney and headed for the ambulance.

The other medic verified the two gunmen were dead then stopped in front of Nelson.

"We'll call the coroner's ambulance to pick the dead ones up," he said.

"I've got the crime team coming," Nelson said. "They'll have to wait until they're done."

"You can take that up with them when they get here," the medic said and moved on toward his ambulance.

A crowd was gathering in front of the alley. "What's going on in there?" someone yelled from the crowd.

"Call for back up, Sid," Nelson said. "We may need them to get out of here."

"Okay, I'll see what I can do in the meantime." Sid walked to the street, cautioning everyone to stay out of the alley.

"He's going to be a good cop," Nelson said.

"Yeah, I think so, too," I said.

Henry, the whores and the little bowling man were standing beside the backdoor, staring.

Sergeant Nelson looked their way and said, "You see what happened here?"

"Those two," Henry said, pointing at the two dead men, "were trying to kill everybody, but Tommy mowed them down."

"Who's Tommy?" Nelson asked.

"He's talking about me, but that's not exactly what happened," I said.

"I see. Well, all of you go back inside but don't leave, someone will be in to ask you questions," Nelson said.

They all started nodding like bobblehead dolls and walked back inside.

"I'll have to ask you to stick around, Tommy, I need a statement for the crime team," Nelson said, grinning.

"Don't let that Tommy thing get out," I said.

"You and Modele the only ones involved?" he asked.

"No, Darcie and my client, who was apparently the target, were also here."

"Were they hit?"

"No, I had to get them out of here before some more bad guys showed up."

"The crime team boys aren't going to like that, Mecana. You know better," he said.

"It was what I had to do."

Nelson told Sid to mark off where Modele fell and around the dead guys.

Sid nodded and did as he was told.

My phone rang and I quickly took it out of my pocket, thinking something may have happened to Darcie. It was Emily.

"Who's that?" Nelson asked.

"It's my daughter Emily. Excuse me a minute." I walked a few steps and answered the phone. "Emily, you picked a bad time. I can't talk now. I'll have to call you later."

"Are you going to get my car?" she asked.

"Yes, we'll talk about it when I have time."

"When will that be?"

"As soon as I can. I have to go." I hung up. "Sorry about that," I told Nelson.

"It's okay, got kids myself."

I expected my phone to ring again any minute, Morgan always followed her sister's lead.

Instead, I heard another siren on the way.

51

CHAPTER 7

To my surprise I didn't get a phone call from Morgan, but something much worse.

Chandler and Blount arrived. They thought they were the old TV team Starsky and Hutch, when in reality they were more like Peter Sellers' Inspector Clouseau. They had good intentions, but they could screw up a train wreck. You never knew what they would do. Usually it was something off the wall they probably saw in a movie.

Robert Chandler was a tall, thin white guy with a moustache and pointed chin. He had a wife and four kids. It took him twenty years to make it to a plainclothes detective, and he was barely hanging on to that.

Kimber Blount, on the other hand, was the smarter of the two and the one that kept Chandler out of trouble. He was younger than Chandler, single, black, with a gym rat body.

They walked up and looked at the two dead guys. "You do that Mecana?" Chandler asked.

"I had some help. You two assigned or just happen to answer a call?"

"I think you better give me your piece," Blount said and held out his hand, working his fingers back and forth.

I reluctantly handed him my Glock. "My client was the target. The dead guys were pros," I said.

"Both of those guys were shot in the back, Mecana," Chandler said. "There's blood running out of holes in their backs. How could they shoot you with their backs to you?"

"You see the weapons they were carrying, detective?" Nelson said.

"Nelson, you stay out of this. We're in charge here," Blount said.

"Take me downtown and let me talk to Verves," I said.

"You're in no position to be giving orders, Mecana. You quit, remember," Blount said. "We'll decide what to do, not you."

"And what's that?" I said.

"We wait for the forensic guys to get here and you tell us how all this went down," Chandler said. "Where's your client now?"

"I can't tell you that," I said.

"Then we we'll have to arrest you for obstructing justice," Blount said.

"Then do it." I was like Brer Rabbit; throw me in the briar patch. Plus, I knew I would get to talk to Verves.

Chandler took his handcuffs off his belt and motioned for me to turn around. He cuffed me and pulled out his Miranda card.

"That's not necessary," I said. "I know my rights."

"You never were very good at following police procedure, Mecana. I am," he said and continued reading from the Miranda card.

A police van pulled up to the alley and three men got out wearing white coats over their uniforms and nylon gloves, carrying plastic bags and blood syringes. The crime team had arrived.

The coroner's ambulance stopped behind them and two men dressed in blue scrubs got out and wheeled two gurneys with body bags over to the dead men.

"Hey you, coroner guy," one of the crime team men yelled. "Wait up. We have to do our job before you move them."

"Then do it," the medic said. "We want to get out of here."

Chandler escorted me to the cruiser and sat me down in the back seat. "Stay put," he said and went back to talk to the crime team. A few minutes later he returned with Blount.

Chandler motioned the cruiser through the crowd, waved at Sergeant Nelson as he passed and hauled ass for the police station.

Morgan still hadn't called. I was getting worried.

CHAPTER 8

Chandler, true to his word, followed procedure to the letter; with everything from taking my mugshot to emptying my pockets. I asked to keep my phone but he wouldn't let me. They locked me in a holding cell and walked away. Obscenities were written all over the walls, some in blood. I noticed four different colors of paint where the wall touched the concrete floor.

It was a weekly task to cover the filth with any kind of paint that was available. The inmates would carve their trash with anything that would scratch the surface.

When Verves showed up I was still reading the wall.

"Unlock the cell," Verves said and handed the jailer a paper. The jailer looked at the paper, nodded and complied. "I heard Modele is in bad shape, and you had Darcie and Mrs. Kane leave the crime scene. Not good."

"I had to get them out of harm's way," I said. "You tell anyone besides Modele what we were doing?"

"No," Verves said.

"It was self-defense," I said.

"Did you tell Chandler and Blount you were there to have your client talk to Modele?"

"I never got the chance."

"You're putting me in a bind, Mecana."

"Sorry," I said, "but this was like a mob hit."

"Maybe they were," Verves said.

"No IDs, maybe fingerprints will tell us who they were," I said.

"I'll start with that," Verves said. "I convinced a judge you contacted me and was there to see Modele when the shit hit the fan; and that you acted in self-defense. You'll have to appear in court later to clear the record but you're free to go for now, as long as you promise me you will bring Mrs. Kane in for a talk."

"Deal," I said. "I'd like to get a bio on the Kanes and a copy of the autopsy, if you'll arrange it."

"Don't have time?" Verves said.

"I can pick it up," I said.

Verves looked at me and sighed. "I'll see what I can do. You have twenty-four hours to bring in Mrs. Kane."

"Thanks," I said and walked away.

I stopped by the claims room and picked up my Glock and other items.

One thing I didn't see in the room was the box from The Mutilator case.

I caught a taxi and had him do some double-backs before it felt like we were clear. When we finally headed for the lake house I called Morgan. I explained it would be a while but we would go to Disneyland as soon as I could get the time. She was always inclined to take me at my word whereas Emily wasn't. I suspected it was her mother's fault.

Henry's refurbished Ford and my truck were sitting in the driveway. I wondered what kind of reaction the rental company was going to have when they saw their car.

The taxi stopped. I got out and paid him. It was time to have a come-to-Jesus meeting with Miss Candy.

I called Darcie when I got to the door. "I'm here," I said.

Darcie opened the door, Beretta in her hand.

"Where's Candy?" I asked.

"In the kitchen, trying to force down a TV dinner," she said.

We walked into the kitchen and Candy was sitting at a long dining table with a glass of wine and a napkin thrown over her microwave meal.

"Mecana, I can't eat this slop. Let me order us some food from Frailer."

"At two hundred dollars a plate?" I said.

"Whatever, I'll pay for it. I'm hungry," she said.

"We have to talk first," I said. "And you're going to have to talk to the cops again."

She stood up, picked up her wine glass and drank what was left.

"Anything else you should tell us?" I said.

"I figured if I told you the truth you wouldn't help me. But I guess I have to."

"That would help," I said.

She picked up the bottle of wine, poured her glass full and drank half of it before sitting it back on the table.

"You'll find out sooner or later. Might as well tell you the whole thing," she said.

"We're listening," Darcie said.

"I was a runaway at sixteen."

"From where?" Darcie asked.

"Atlanta, Georgia. My mother was a drug addict and prostitute. I never knew who my father was. I don't think she did, either. I got tired of fighting off her pimp, so I made my way to Dallas and took up my mother's profession as a freelancer to survive. She died from an overdose three months later."

"You have any more family?" Darcie asked.

"Not that I know of," she said.

"What's your mother's married and maiden names?" Darcie said. "I'll check it out."

"Adele Parnell," she said. "She was never married.

"A couple years after she died I met Ashton. His chauffer was cruising around one night, looking for a girl for Ashton and he saw me. He asked if I would like to make a thousand dollars. I said yes and that's how it all started.

"Ashton was amused by our names together. We had sex in a hotel suite that night. Afterwards, he asked if he could hypnotize me; told me he was a medical hypnotist and would give me another thousand dollars to let him. I thought what the hell and the next thing I knew, I woke up hours later naked in the bedroom."

"You don't remember what you did while you were hypnotized?" Darcie said.

"No."

"What happened after that?" Darcie said.

"He said he would like for me to stay with him; that he could help me overcome some problems he discovered while I was under hypnosis."

"Like what," I said.

"While I was under, he said I revealed my mother's psychotic abuse. He also said he could change my perception of who I was for the better, with more treatments."

"Did he?" Darcie said.

"Yes. He freed my mind through hypnosis to experience insight into my problems and a state of mind to understand how I could change my life.

"We were married that year. He's twenty years older than I am."

"Did he tell you what you did while hypnotized," Darcie said.

"No. He explained he conditioned me to have spontaneous amnesia after each session; thought it best I didn't know."

"You need to tell the cops what you just told us," I said.

"No. I'm not sure I should have even told you," she said.

"It won't go any further," Darcie said. "If that's what you want."

"No one," Candy said.

"Anything else you want to tell us?" Darcie said.

"Nothing I can think of," she said.

"That's an incredible story," Darcie said.

"I promised Verves I would bring you in for questioning," I said. "We'll get you something to eat on the way."

"I thought I didn't have to go in."

"The bowling alley incident changed all that."

"What will they do to me?" she said.

"Darcie's a lawyer, she can represent you. I don't think it's the cops you have to worry about, anyway. I'm beginning to think there's more to this than money. When you have that kind of firepower involved, it's something besides revenge."

"I wouldn't know. By the way, Ashton's body is coming home tomorrow morning," Candy said. "The funeral will be at Memorial Gardens at 3:30 tomorrow afternoon."

"We'll be there to protect you," I said. "Who's coming?"

"I didn't invite anyone," she said.

"Landon Fritz won't be there?"

No," she said. "He may be the one who's trying to kill me."

"You don't think it's Fillmore anymore?"

"Landon is next in line on Ashton's will to inherit his fortune. If I'm gone he would get the billons Ashton left."

"Why didn't you tell us this before?" Darcie said.

"I don't know," she said.

"I think you do, you just didn't want us to know. Why?"

"I forgot," she said. "That's all."

"You're too smart to forget something like that," I said.

"I did, that's the only reason," she said.

"Doubt that. We'll talk again. Let's go talk to Verves now," I said.

When we walked in the homicide department, Officers Chandler and Blount gave us a fixed stare as we made our way to Verves' glass office. When he saw us, he stood up and we walked in.

"This is Candy Kane, Chief," I said. Candy nodded and Verves did the same.

We sat and I noticed Chandler and Blount were still staring at us. "Chief, you got something for them to do? I feel like we're in a zoo in this glass office."

Verves looked up at them and waved his hand toward the outside door. They gave us a smirk, stood up from their desks and walked out.

Verves walked around his desk and looked at Candy. "I'm sorry about your husband, Mrs. Kane. We have to ask you some questions, for the record. Darcie, are you her attorney?"

"Yes," Darcie said.

"Mecana, why don't you get you a cup of coffee and mingle with your old comrades while we do this," Verves said.

Thinking of the coffee made me sick, but I nodded and stood up.

"Okay, ladies, if you will follow me," Verves said, "we'll get this over with."

Candy and Darcie stood up. Verves picked up a folder and a large manila envelope from his desk. He handed me the envelope and placed the folder under his arm.

"I think that's what you wanted, Mecana," he said.

Candy and Darcie followed Verves out of his office down the hall to the interrogation room. I sat down to wait and opened the envelope.

CHAPTER 9

The first thing I noticed when I pulled the contents out of the envelope was one of the crime scene pictures of Ashton Kane. It showed him lying on the bed face-down, a sheet pulled over the lower part of his body with his legs and feet sticking out. He was naked when he was killed by four 9mm slugs that could have been from a small hand gun. It was also the preferred choice of pistol for many women.

Candy was licensed to carry a handgun but she wasn't there to do it; unless we could prove otherwise. Verves and his bunch couldn't.

A 5"x7" picture was clipped to the page; showing Mr. Kane in a white coat with a nametag and a stethoscope around his neck. He was a good-looking man with blue eyes, a full head of combed-back black hair with a touch of gray that gave him a distinguished look. A note on the bottom of the picture listed his height as 6′ 2″, weight at 200 lbs. and age as 48 years old.

According to the files, his parents were killed in a plane crash on their way to a business trip in Florida for the bank where they both worked. Luckily for Ashton, he was being taken care of by his aunt so he could play a little league game that day. He was ten years old when it happened, and spent the rest of his childhood in the care of his aunt.

He was turned down for a full academic scholarship to medical school because he was not active in any extra-curricular activities benefiting the country or community required for the scholarship, even though he was a straight-A student.

He had been arrested for assault and battery for beating up a kid in college after a hazing attempt and was then considered an undesirable by all the other fraternities he attempted to join.

He was also arrested three times for soliciting prostitution after the women filed complaints because of his unusual behavior.

One of the women claimed he hypnotized her to do weird sex things and another one said she was locked in a dark room where he made her watch a video of people having sex for hours and later "tested" her on it. Since no evidence was found, the school only suspended him for a year before he returned to graduate at the top of his class.

A federal charge of fraud was filed three years ago by an Edward Fillmore but Kane had been acquitted of all charges. There was no mention of any lasting relationships with any women other than Candy. Not exactly an all-American boy, but a huge success with an eye for the oldest profession.

Candy was listed as the wife of a doctor and a socialite charity fundraiser.

Her name and her mother's name were as she said. A marriage license to Ashton Kane revealed her maiden name and a rap sheet on her mother's prostitution and drug charges, but Candy had never been booked on any charges.

I heard a door close, looked up and saw Verves and the ladies coming my way. I stuffed the contents back in the envelope and followed them back into Verve's office.

"Have a seat," Verves said.

We sat down and waited for him to speak.

"Mrs. Kane, you said you were in Dallas when your husband was murdered and we have nothing to prove otherwise. But that doesn't mean we can dismiss all interest in you until we confirm other people had the motive and opportunity to kill your husband. We will also have to explore your past in more detail before we can conclude our investigation."

"Chief," Darcie said, "you have personal information and will certainly obtain more in your investigation that we don't want in the press. I want to request you give us the opportunity to prevent private matters from going public."

"That depends," Verves said. "I may be able to do that, but if my boss says they have to be made public there's not much I can do."

"I understand that, but I also know we can sue for invasion of privacy if the information is not relative to the case."

"I'll keep that in mind. We can talk first," Verves said. "Mrs. Kane, again, let me express my sympathy for the loss of your husband. We will keep you posted on any developments in the case."

"Thank you," Candy said. "Chief Verves, I've come a long way from my old life. My background would damage my status now if it is made public. Please consider that for me."

"I'll do what I can," he said.

"May we go now?" Candy asked.

"Yes. Here's a parking pass so you won't have to pay," he said and handed me the pass.

I stood up and shook hands with Verves. "Thanks, Chief," I said, gesturing toward the envelope. "If you find out who was trying to kill us, let me know please."

Verves nodded. Darcie and Candy said goodbye and we left.

We stopped at Brogans on the way home. The chef was familiar with Tibetan Highland Asian Chicken and prepared Candy a gourmet dinner to go. He said DeMax was fired for trying to seduce the manager's wife.

We headed back to the lake house. Candy poured some wine, ate about half of the dinner and retreated to the bedroom with a fresh bottle, saying she was going to get drunk and not to bother her.

Darcie and I found a steak TV dinner. We finished it off and sat down in the living room after feeding the fish.

"Well, Sherlock, what do we do now?" Darcie asked.

"Verves gave me a bio and autopsy of Ashton Kane," I said. "The crime scene picture looked like there may have been some sex going on when Kane was murdered. He had a record of arrests when he was in college for sexual perversions; and one prostitute claimed she was hypnotized by Kane. Sound familiar?" I opened the envelope and handed Darcie the picture.

"Yeah, it does look like he was in a compromising position. The spots on the bed could be semen." She shuffled through the other files. "He wasn't allowed into any fraternities, either. Looks like he worked his way through college. Must have been a loner; maybe some mental problems himself."

"They don't have a normal husband/wife relationship, that's for sure."

"Check the airlines for a round-trip ticket to New York in Candy's name the same night her husband was murdered. I'll have a look at the car. It's supposed to have a bullet hole in the window."

"I'll check the phone calls," Darcie said.

"We need something. We keep running into blank walls."

I picked up the keys to Candy's car but I gave Darcie back the keys to the Kanes' penthouse and his office. "I'd hate to break in."

"I'll go check," Darcie said.

"I'll call DeMax and get him to stay with you while I'm gone," I said. "I'm sure he could use the money. Just make sure he stays away from Candy."

"I'll tell him something like, 'You bother her and I'll shoot your balls off,'" she said.

"That should do it," I grinned. "I'm going by the house to clean up and check my machine to see if the kids called. Run a bio on Fillmore for me and send it to the house."

"You got it, Sherlock," she said.

"We'll have to go to the funeral with Candy tomorrow. It's the perfect place for an ambush."

CHAPTER 10

After taking a shower by myself I put on a blue pullover sweater and a pair of Dockers Darcie bought me. I was buckling my Glock holster when I noticed something off…my roll of quarters was gone from the dresser. Darcie may have stuck them away somewhere and deprived me of a legal weapon.

I checked the machine. No messages from Emily or Morgan. I called my daughters to let them know I was tied up for a while but had the money to get them what they wanted as soon as I finished my case.

Emily suggested I send the money to her mother and let her help buy the car and then they would take Morgan to Disneyland. I told her I would think about it, although I knew I had no intentions of letting my ex-wife's new boy-friend play daddy.

Darcie called before I could call her. She told me to check my computer; she had sent me the bio on Edward Fillmore.

Looking over it, I read he resided in one of the more up-scale buildings and was the CEO of a financial firm. He was forty years old and a Harvard grad with a PhD in Economics. Fillmore also had two kids but was divorced because he was unfaithful to his wife with Candy Kane, according to the divorce papers.

The only note listed on his medical treatment was, "Patient escapes into numbness to forget unpleasant events he has no solution for, and is best served by medical hypnotism to prevent further mind-altering thoughts."

So that explained why he was being hypnotized.

He had filed a lawsuit against Ashton Kane for ten million dollars, claiming Kane hypnotized him to transfer ten million dollars from his account. The case was thrown out of court due to lack of evidence.

I checked the marquee outside the building, this was the right place.

Inside, I stepped into the elevator with a group of well-dressed white-haired men who were probably executives of companies in the building. I got off on the tenth floor and saw a brass sign across the hall with an arrow pointing to my left.

When I walked in, a redheaded secretary was sitting at the desk next to a door labeled 'CEO Edward G Fillmore.'

"May I help you?" she asked.

"Yes, I need to talk to Mr. Fillmore," I said and handed her my newly-printed business card.

"Is Mr. Fillmore expecting you?"

"No ma'am, but I think he will want to see me. It's about the murder of Ashton Kane."

"I don't think so, Mr. Mecana. He gave me instructions not to let anyone in if it concerned Mr. Kane."

"I'm not leaving until I do."

She stood up and stepped in front of the door to his office. "I'll call the police. You're trespassing."

"I could also push you out of the way and go in before they get here."

She stared at me and didn't move.

"Wait here," she finally said, quickly opening and closing the door as she went in.

Seconds later, Fillmore burst out of his office looking at my card, jumpy as a bullfrog.

He was a tall, good-looking man wearing an expensive blue suit and red tie. He had thick black hair, dark brown eyes and a mustache.

"Mr. Mecana, take your ass outta here," he said. "I know about Kane's murder. I have an iron-clad alibi. He accused me of trying to fuck his wife and used his profession to take advantage of me. The emotional problems I have could never lead to murdering anyone. Now get out of my office before I have Miss Wingate call the cops."

"She's already threatened to do that," I said. "We can do this the easy way or the hard way, Mr. Fillmore. I have no desire to cause you further trouble, but I need the truth.

You better make damn sure that's what you're telling me."

He rubbed his hands together and grimaced like he was in pain. "Okay. Come in my office."

He motioned for me to go through the open door. I walked in and he followed and sat behind his desk. I sat down in a chair in front of his desk.

"I was in London attending a business meeting when he was murdered," Fillmore said. "Lots of witnesses. I may be glad someone killed him but it wasn't me. His wife tried to recruit me to obtain information on several of my clients for market deals, using herself as the reward. I admit I thought it over but changed my mind. Nothing happened. He's an evil mental case and she's an evil whore. I think they're the perfect pair for the devil. That's the truth as I see it. Now get out."

He got to his feet, hurried to the door and opened it, waiting for me to leave. He had been so blunt it seemed to be the truth. I got up and walked out the door.

"Another time," I said to the secretary as I left the office.

I still had the keys Darcie gave me so I decided to check out Kane's office for another look.

When I arrived and opened the door the alarm didn't go off this time. The office was in a state of disarray. It had been ransacked after I went through it the first time.

I noticed some of the things I remembered had been moved; like the replica Maltese Falcon from one of Bogart's movies was sitting on a table now instead of the marble desk, and a bottom desk drawer now open that I didn't leave that way, and a painting that looked like an original Picasso was gone from the wall behind his desk. Vandals, murderers, or both. Maybe someone who knew what they were looking for found it.

All the files were gone and either the sneaks or the police had them. I had been through the files before they disappeared but didn't remember anything suspicious, except for the fact there wasn't a file on Fillmore. Probably destroyed by Kane to keep it from the courts. Fillmore had denied any involvement with Candy but seemed too nervous for it not to have happened.

The only interesting tidbit I found was an index file card file on Kane's desk with the words 'Song for Pons, Turkey soon.' Turkey was capitalized; did he mean the country?

I was getting a headache and decided after I checked the car I would skip the penthouse until tomorrow. I stuck the index card in my pocket, locked the office and left.

I remembered the parking space number because she said it was the same as her age - 28. But it wasn't there. Someone must have towed it away. Or, on second thought, maybe she drove it away. Most people have two sets of keys. But she'd been with us since we took her case.

I scouted the hotel for info about the car. No one knew anything about it. Called all the local towing companies but none of them knew anything, either.

Would need to have another talk with Candy about the damn car. My headache was getting worse.

As I drove back to the lake house I thought about the index card, Fillmore, the doctor's funeral, Candy, and her car for a while; then decided I needed a thought break and switched to my girls.

I was most worried about what Emily said. I wondered if that was what she really thought or if it was her mother putting thoughts in her head so she could take her scumbag of a boyfriend with them to Disneyland in Emily's new car.

I thought about calling Emily but decided it wouldn't help and called Darcie instead.

She said, "DeMax was there but said he didn't make a pass at the manager's wife, she was just mad at him because he didn't."

"Not sure I believe that," I said.

"Lots of calls between Kane and a Landon Fritz about everything from golf to Candy," Darcie said. "Sounded like they're buddies. In the Candy discussion they were talking about her mental and hypnosis status and about a song for an Alonza Pons from Turkey. No idea what they meant by that. Only info I found on Pons is he is the head of an executive committee to the UN from Turkey."

"That's interesting," I said. "I found an index card in Kane's office with the words song, Pons and Turkey on it. That's a match. You got an address on Fritz?"

"Yes," she said.

"I'm beginning to think Kane was using his profession to take advantage of people and Candy was using her former profession to help make it happen."

"I'll ask Candy about Fritz," Darcie said. "She said the three of them had spent a lot of time together visiting foreign countries."

"I don't think Candy is telling us everything. And Fillmore had a good alibi but it really doesn't matter," I said. "He could have hired the goons who came after us. He's a pretty sick puppy. I'm on my way back to the lake house now. I'll be there in about thirty minutes."

DeMax met me at the door.

"Hey Mecana," he said. "They're in the bedroom. The pretty lady drank herself to sleep so Miss Darcie is watching over her."

"How long has she been out?" I said.

"About two hours," DeMax said. "I offered to stay with her, but Miss Darcie said she would."

I walked into the bedroom. Candy was lying on the bed in silk pajamas, her legs drawn up into the fetal position, her closed eyelids flickering rapidly; must be having a bad dream.

"Hope you didn't hypnotize her," I said and grinned.

"You're not as funny as you think you are," Darcie said. "She's been making gurgling noises in her sleep."

I glanced at two large empty wine bottles on the bed-side table. I picked up one of the bottles and looked at the label.

"Just paying for two bottles of this would make me drunk," I said. "I'm having to deal with my two daughters. They're being brainwashed by their mother with the help of her dumbass boyfriend. Might have to go kick his ass."

I didn't realize DeMax was standing behind me in the doorway until he spoke.

"Just give me a name and I'll make the motherfucker wish he was somebody else, Mecana."

"I appreciate the offer but I need you here," I told him.

DeMax nodded and walked away.

"Never thinks about his language," Darcie said.

"Hope I didn't hurt his feelings," I said.

"DeMax is a martial arts expert," Darcie said. "Saw it in his records."

"No shit? Maybe I'll change my mind."

"Kind of sneaky," Darcie said.

"I don't care," I said and sat down on the corner of the bed. Candy moaned, turned over and flipped her hand on my crotch.

"She better be asleep," Darcie said.

"She is...I think," I said and moved her hand.

"You resent the boyfriend because he replaced you, don't you?" Darcie said.

"I resent him because he's an asshole."

"You still care for her?"

"I thought you were a lawyer, not a psychologist."

"Just trying to help."

"Well, you're not. What kind of martial arts expert is DeMax?"

"I don't know, Mecana, it just said martial arts. Once you get your mind on something it never leaves until you're satisfied with it, does it?"

"Nope."

"The insurance guy called me," she said. "I told him we would send his money back, we didn't have time to work on his case. He was pretty pissed."

"Changing the subject?" I said.

"I am," she said. "I like the clothes you have on."

"An inquisitive lady bought them for me." I stood up and struck a pose. "Did you see my roll of quarters on the dresser?"

She smiled. "No. I think it's time to wake up Candy and escort her to the shower," she said. "You can't come."

"Party pooper. I'll go talk to DeMax," I said.

DeMax was watching reruns of Hap and Leonard in the living room when I walked in. I sat down on the couch beside him.

"Thanks for offering to take care of the boyfriend but I think I'll let it go for now. Darcie told me you were a martial arts expert. I never knew."

"Maybe not an expert, but I have a black belt."

"I don't remember you using any martial arts stuff when we arrested you as a suspect in The Mutilator case."

"Would have got me in more trouble for kickin' your ass," DeMax said.

"Not to mention my broken bones. The guy's a jerk but I'm going to need you for a lot of other things, if you want to stick around."

"Fine with me," he said. "Got nothing else to do."

"Okay, you can help us solve this case."

He smiled. "You mean that?"

"I do," I said. "I'll even pay you."

"How much?" he asked.

"Two thousand a week," I said. "Until we solve the case. Won't be long I hope."

"Room and board, too?"

"I can do that, plus a bonus when we solve the case."

"Sounds fair."

"Good," I said. "We agree then?"

"We do." DeMax stretched out on the couch and went back to watching TV.

The name Landon Fritz kept popping up in my head. Maybe he could shed some light on what the hell was going on with the 'song' shit.

I glanced at the TV. "Two good ol' Texas boys getting their due."

CHAPTER 11

The next morning I was waiting for Candy to wake up so I could get more information on Landon Fritz. I had also been trying to learn as much as possible about hypnotism on the internet. It all kind of ran together for me. I always thought of it as entertainment, and never took it seriously until I found out doctors had been studying hypnotism for over two hundred years to treat emotional, physical and mental illnesses. Some even claimed they could improve intelligence with hypnotism.

DeMax walked in wearing a #4 Dallas Cowboys jersey.

I was eating cereal. "Get you something to eat, DeMax."

"Too early for me. I'll run down to McDonalds later," he said. "Miss Darcie said I can't have a gun when you go to New York."

"Well, not legally, but if someone breaks in you can use one in self-defense."

"You going to leave one?" DeMax said.

"I'll leave a .45 over there by the aquarium," I said.

"How long are you going to be gone?"

"We have to go to the doctor's funeral today and then I need you to hold down the fort for a day or two while I'm in New York. Call the cops if someone comes around who shouldn't."

"I will," he said.

"Hopefully, all you'll have to do is watch television and feed the fish for me."

"Big job," DeMax said and turned on the TV.

We left the lake house around two that afternoon and headed for Memorial Gardens.

When the hearse arrived, two men reeled out the coffin, sat it on a stand beside the grave and backed off. I didn't see a preacher.

"Is anyone going to give him a send off, Candy?"

"No. I just have to certify he's buried and go by the bank to have his money signed over to me. You can be witnesses."

A man on a backhoe showed up. Three men lowered his coffin into the grave and the man on the backhoe covered it up. The shortest and coldest funeral I ever saw.

"Take me to the bank." Candy pitched a single flower on the grave and we left without another word.

Darcie and I parked outside the bank with Candy and went inside. We sat outside the bank president's office with the door open so we could keep an eye out.

She conducted her business. We heard bits and pieces of their conversation. She was asking him to close the accounts and give her the cash. The president looked at her like he was totally surprised at what she wanted him to do and shook his head no. She stood up and shook a finger at him and he sat back down, wrote something on a paper handed it to her. She signed it, pitched it back to him and walked out of the office.

"Don't ask, let's go," Candy said. "You don't have to sign anything."

On the way back to the lake house, we stopped by Brogans and picked up another special meal for Candy. When we got to the bungalow she poured a glass of wine and ate most of her meal.

"I'm going to get my stuff shipped to France and make arrangements to leave the day after tomorrow," she said. "I'll put another hundred grand in your account and you'll be done with your job."

"For whatever reason, people are still looking for you. We'll have to let the cops know what you're doing," I said.

"Since you put it that way, forget the hundred grand. I'll take care of myself from here on out." She drained her wine glass.

"You can do what you want, but you're not getting killed on our time. We'll keep a watch until you're gone. Unless the cops want you," I said.

"Suit yourself," she said and walked away with her glass and a fresh bottle of wine; Darcie following with a TV dinner.

DeMax and I took ours into the living room to watch television; Dallas Football was coming on in the next thirty minutes. We sat down and devoured our TV dinner just in time for football.

A roaring airplane-like sound shook the walls of the house. We thought it was the TV for a second. I looked out the window and saw a monster truck with huge Caterpillar-size tires bouncing down the driveway at an incredible speed, headed straight for the house.

A man in the passenger seat leaned out the window and started firing an automatic weapon at the house.

We hit the floor.

I yelled "Stay down!" as loud as I could and crawled faster than a snake toward the hallway. DeMax was right behind me following suit.

We barely made it to the hallway before the monster truck crashed through the wall, sending debris flying everywhere. The driver and another man jumped out, spraying the room with bullets.

I heard a woman scream and knew it was Candy. I jumped up in the hallway and ran as fast as I could toward the bedroom, DeMax in hot pursuit.

Darcie came running out of the bedroom holding her Berretta, Candy right behind her naked and wet.

"Go back," I told them.

They turned around and I saw a black bird sitting on a limb tattooed on Candy's butt. We all ran into the bedroom. I grabbed a suitcase on the bed, smashed a window with it and we climbed out with the burglar alarm screaming at us. We ran to my truck, me hoping the suitcase I was carrying held some clothes for Candy.

I opened a back door, threw in the suitcase and Darcie and Candy got in and hugged the floorboard. I started the truck, peeled out and headed for the gate.

DeMax jumped on his bike and slung dirt everywhere as he took off.

The two killers ran out the door firing at us, bullets ripping holes in Henry's parked truck and mine as I drove through the open gate to the street. All those holes in my truck were going to end my love affair with it. And I would have to find Henry a new one now, too.

DeMax wheeled his bike up beside the truck. "Everybody okay?" he asked.

Both women answered yes and I nodded at him.

"Let me borrow your bike," I told DeMax. "I have to get them before they come after us."

"You want me to go with you?" DeMax said.

"No, stay with them and take off if you see anyone besides me coming."

DeMax jumped off the bike. I jumped on, made a circle and headed back to the house.

As I wheeled through the hole in the wall, I saw the two men walking back toward the monster truck. I went full-throttle and jerked the front wheel up; it deflected some bullets and caught one man on top of his head, crushing his skull. He dropped his weapon and fell to the floor, blood streaming down the side of his head.

I brought the wheel down and dove off the bike, letting it slide across the floor to the other man, cutting his feet out from under him. He hit the floor and lost his machine pistol. I fired as quickly as I could. He yelled and crawled toward the gun. I emptied my Glock in him and blood surrounded him like a red rug.

A patrol car shot through the gate, lights flashing and siren screaming, and spun to a stop in front of the hole in the wall. I tossed the empty Glock to the floor and sat down with my hands behind my head. Two cops jumped out with their weapons drawn and ran inside.

"Don't move," one of them said.

"Don't shoot," I replied. "My weapon's on the floor in front of you. I'm unarmed."

"Stretch out on the floor, put your hands behind your back," the other said.

I did what I was told and a cop with sergeant stripes and 'Knowles' on his nametag handcuffed me. The other one was named Sawyer. He picked up my Glock and the other weapons while Knowles checked the dead men.

"You know them?" Knowles asked.

"No, I'm an ex-cop. Chief Verves knows me. Call him," I said.

"Stay where you are," Sergeant Knowles said.

From a worm's-eye view, I saw another patrol car appear, then another; lights flashing and sirens blasting from all of them. My truck roared up behind them.

"That's my people in the truck, Sergeant, don't shoot."

They all exited the truck with their hands up. Candy was now wearing pajamas, the bird tattoo now out of sight.

The cops shoved them to the ground and handcuffed them as a small crowd gathered at the gate.

The cops helped me up and led me out of the house to a cruiser.

"Are you alright?" Darcie called out.

"Yeah, you?" I yelled back, competing with the sirens.

"We're okay," she shouted back.

They put us in the cruisers. A crime scene patrol and coroner's ambulance drove up as we left the property.

CHAPTER 12

They put me and DeMax in a cell together and took Darcie and Candy to the women's jail across the street to sort out everything.

Verves showed up two hours later wearing jeans and a police t-shirt.

"Mecana, you're beginning to be a real pain in the ass."

"Seems like somebody up there don't like us," I said.

"I stopped by the morgue," Verves said. "They look like Swiss cheese. You know them?"

"Let me guess, they didn't have any ID, either," I said.

"Nothing. I'll see if I can get bail set and get the info over to Darcie, too."

"Thanks," I said.

"Behave yourself, Mecana." He walked away, a guard following him out.

"He likes you," DeMax said. "Are we gonna get out?"

"Maybe," I said.

"I need a gun," DeMax said. "I never got a chance to shoot back."

"You don't have a license," I said.

"Won't make any difference when I'm dead."

"Good point. I'll see what I can do."

The next day, Darcie walked in with a paper in her hand; a gray-haired overweight turnkey with a keychain attached to his belt following her. He stuck a key in the lock and opened our cell, and motioned for us to come out without a word.

"Where's Candy?" I asked.

"I'll tell you later," Darcie said. "Let's just get out of here."

When we walked outside Darcie led us to a new truck and handed me the keys. It was the same make and model as the one that got shot up.

"You bought a new truck," Darcie said.

"I did?" I said.

"Yeah the other one had too many bullet holes to fix. I got you another like the one you were in love with."

"Cool," DeMax said.

"Good and bad," I said. "My damn insurance premiums are going to go through the roof. And I have to get Henry a truck."

"Never promised you a rose garden," Darcie said.

"I always smell flowers when you speak," I said.

"Well isn't that sweet. You must be glad to get out of jail," Darcie said.

"Where's Candy?"

"Deposit your butt in the truck," she said. "DeMax, you can ride up front."

I got in and there was Candy, sitting in the back seat.

"Here I am," she said. "As you can see, the cops don't want me. Find me a place to pee then take me back to my place to pack, I'm leaving today."

"There's a station across the street," DeMax said. "I got to go, too."

"Make it quick," I said and pulled into the station's parking lot. "Looks like the restrooms are inside. What about you, Darcie?"

"I'm good," she said.

"Go with Candy," I said.

"You think I need a chaperone to pee?" Candy said.

"I don't want anyone to kill you on our watch," I said. We got out and headed to the restrooms.

When DeMax and I walked in the men's room, two big men wearing suits followed in behind us. I could see them in the mirrors. They stopped in the middle of the floor and drew automatics out of their coats.

"Don't move," the older-looking man said and motioned for us to move against the wall. He placed his revolver against my head and removed the Glock from my shoulder holster while the younger one patted us down.

"Stay put you two," the older one said. "You poke your head out that door and we'll blow it clean off." They bolted from the room in a run.

We stopped at the door but it wouldn't open; they had pushed a vending machine against it. We heard a woman screaming outside. We could see through a crack in the door they were carrying Candy to their car. We shoved the door open but they were already gone. We ran into the ladies restroom where Darcie was crawling out from under a locked stall.

"They took Candy," she said.

"What did they look like?" I said.

"Two white men in suits. One had a shaved head and the other one was smaller and thinner with a beard."

"Same ones who came after us."

"Damn, they're fast," DeMax said.

"Let's go," I said. "Maybe we can catch up."

We started for the door when a little man with shaggy blonde hair ran in with a .38 in his hand. According to the nametag on his black fast food shirt, his name was George and he was the manager at the fast food place inside the station.

"I called the police," George said, waving the .38 at us. "The other ones got away but you and Sambo ain't."

DeMax looked at me with a fire in his eyes.

"Go ahead," I said.

DeMax jumped toward the little man, kicking the gun out of his hand. He spun around and laid a right cross on his chin so hard he staggered across the restroom, his arms flying around like a windmill. He banged his head on the wall and fell to the floor, out cold.

I picked up his .38 and stuck it in my pocket.

"What's he doing that for?" Darcie asked, staring at DeMax.

"The little man was insulting him," I said.

"Holy shit," she said.

"They take your Berretta?"

"Yes," she said.

"We fucked up, didn't we," DeMax said.

"Yes we did," I said.

We hurried out of the restrooms and into the station.

"Anyone see the car the men put that lady in?" I asked aloud.

Four or five people in the store stopped shopping for a moment and stared at us, but said nothing and went back to shopping.

A young woman behind the counter wearing the same black fast food shirt as George held her hand up like a schoolgirl in class.

"Are you a cop?" she said, looking at me.

"Was at one time, Sally," I said, looking at the name on her shirt.

"Two guys came out of the ladies room carrying a blonde lady, kicking and screaming, with her panties hanging around one ankle about to fall off," she said. "They put her in a white van and took off north down Reilly Street. A big black car followed."

"Do you remember any plate numbers from either one?"

"First two on the van were 16," she said. "That's all I remember."

I reached in my pocket and pulled a hundred dollar bill off my money clip and handed it to her. "You've been a lot of help, Sally. Thanks."

Sergeant Nelson and his young partner drove up beside us in the parking lot as we were headed to the truck.

"Just received a disturbance call," Nelson said. "You have anything to do with it, Mecana?"

I stopped beside my driver-side door for a second as DeMax and Darcie were getting in. "Can't explain now, Nelson. Have to run. My client was kidnapped."

I got in the truck and started the engine. I waved at Nelson and floor-boarded the gas pedal.

CHAPTER 13

The sun dropped out of sight over the next few minutes, making it harder to chase the perpetrators in the dark. If they intended to kill Candy it was done by now. I stopped at a red light and a white van roared by, heading the other direction.

"That was a 16 on the plate, wasn't it," I said. "He's doubling back"

"I saw it," DeMax said.

"I did too," Darcie said. "But we don't know if it's the right one."

I whipped the truck around and followed the van for several miles but didn't see the big black car. The van turned off I-20 onto Highway 49 toward Houston and the black Mercedes appeared almost out of nowhere, following it.

"It's the right van," I said. "When I find a place I can block the van, I will. Darcie, you and DeMax get out of the truck and haul ass when I stop."

"You can't do that," Darcie said. "They probably have all kinds of weapons."

"May be our only chance," I said. "Plus, I've got that manager's .38."

The van changed lanes to the right, headed towards the next exit. I waited for cars to come around me and dropped back a ways. The van made a right at the first street and the Mercedes followed.

"They must still have her. Somebody may want her alive," I said.

The van and the Mercedes made a right turn on Mable Street and headed north. I stayed back a ways, keeping the two vehicles in sight. The van moved over to the right again and, the Mercedes still following, pulled into a lit-up driveway with a big iron gate topped with 1924 SOUTH HALL ST; a rock fence surrounding a two-story brick building.

I drove past the gate and stopped under the shadow of a tree two blocks away and cut the lights and engine.

"What we do now?" DeMax asked.

"We call the FBI. We've got a kidnapping," Darcie said.

In the next instance, a whishing sound crash-busted out both front windows, glass flying all over. The two men we encountered at the station appeared on each side of my truck with AK-47s pointed at us.

"Throw out your weapons or we'll kill you," the bearded one said.

I tossed the .38 out the busted window. "That's all we've got."

"Come on, the rest of it."

"You already have it."

"Get out of the truck," the bearded guy said.

We opened the door and stepped out of the truck. I saw the baseball bat he used to bust the glass laying on the ground. Must be another one on the other side, I thought.

"Give me the keys," the bearded one said.

"They're in the truck," I said.

The shaved-headed one pushed Darcie and DeMax toward the front of the truck with the barrel of his AK-47 and motioned for them to keep walking.

"Go to the gate," he said.

The other one drove the truck up through the gate and cut the engine got off. He threw the keys as far as he could and picked up his AK-47 off the seat.

They opened the front door and walked us into a big room with a long table and eight straight-backed chairs.

"Sit down," the younger one said.

No sooner had we deposited our butts on the chairs than an old white-haired man with a matching white beard walked in smiling.

"Well, if it's not the famous mutilation detective," he said.

"And you look like Landon Fritz. I was going to come see you," I said.

"For a supposedly good cop you're not very good at tailing. We had to double back just so you wouldn't lose us."

"You bastard. Where's Candy?" Darcie said.

"I put her to sleep," Fritz said.

"For good?" I said.

"Heavens, no. I stuck a needle in her. But the night bird will be dead soon."

"Candy's got one tattooed on her butt," Darcie said.

I nodded affirmative.

"Ashton said she had it when they met. She called herself a night bird because of her profession. It conveniently gave him a code name for her."

"A code name for what?" I said.

"Since I'm going to kill you anyway," Fritz said, "what the hell.

"Candy killed whoever Ashton told her to kill; under suggested programming installed over a long period of time from hypnosis. She could blow anyone's brains out without the slightest remorse and wouldn't remember anything after. And with her looks, she never had any trouble getting men alone.

"A perfect assassin."

"That's crazy," I said. "Nobody could do that."

"Ashton ruined it all when he discovered she was having an affair with his private pilot," Fritz told them. "Kane told her what she had been doing for him and that he was going to turn her in to the cops. So she killed him.

"We were paid a million and a half by a terrorist group for a hit that never happened and now they're after us. I told them I would do away with Candy and give them her settlement money from Kane to make things even. I kept her alive to catch you morons."

"Your hit was Pons?" I said.

"How did you know?" Fritz said.

"Found the name on a card."

"She should have done what she was told. I had something else prepared for her if she got away."

"What was that," I said.

"Won't need it now," Fritz said and turned to the two hitmen. "Take them to the Melrose Mine Pit and bury them. I'll take care of our night bird."

Both men nodded and Fritz hurried out the door.

They were going to bury us alive.

The men were standing on each side of us a couple of feet away.

"Let's go," the younger one said, waving his AK-47.

"The three finger plan," I told DeMax.

"But we only did that once," he said.

"Now it'll be twice. Left."

"Right, on three," he said and held up three fingers.

"Under," Darcie said. We nodded.

Both men looked at each other, puzzled by what were doing.

DeMax raised his right arm and held out three fingers. "One," he said and dropped the first finger.

"Stop that," shaved head said and slapped DeMax's hand down. "Get out or we'll kill you right here."

DeMax raised his arm again. "Two," he said and dropped a second finger.

Shaved head swung his weapon at DeMax. He ducked.

"Three," he said and we all charged; myself to the left, DeMax to the right, and Darcie sliding across the floor, hitting their feet and making them lose balance.

DeMax kicked one in the face, knocking his gun out of his hands, and grabbed it on the way to the floor.

I tackled the other one and snatched his weapon as we were going down, then rolled over on top of him and pounded him with the stock several times.

We scrambled to our feet and opened fire. Their bodies looked like a screen door when we stopped. The entire fight lasted less than a minute.

Fritz ran in the doorway, saw what happened and ran out.

We hurried out the door after Fritz. I saw a small statue rocking on a table beside the first door on the right. We pushed up against the wall beside the door and I grabbed the statue off the table and threw it as hard as I could against the door. Three bullets zipped through the door, making holes big enough to see Fritz holding an automatic to Candy's head.

I busted through the door and Fritz grabbed Candy around the neck, stood her up and pushed the automatic tighter against her head.

"Don't shoot, we'll make a deal," I said. "Back out the door without shooting her and we'll let you go. Shoot her and you won't leave the room."

Fritz began to twitch his hand and mock-pulling the trigger on the automatic.

"Candy!" Darcie yelled.

Candy was blurry-eyed and in a daze. She moaned and Fritz tightened his grip on her.

"Wake up," Darcie said while DeMax and I shouted her name.

She groggily shook her head and saw Fritz was holding on to her. She started clawing at him, pulling him to the floor. Fritz let go of her and dropped his automatic. She picked up his gun and fired four quick bullets into his chest, tearing his heart apart. He fell over on his back with a thud beside her.

Darcie dropped down beside Candy, snatched the gun from her and threw it across the room.

"DeMax, go check the rest of this place," I said.

He nodded and hurried out the door, carrying an AK-47.

"Candy, do you know what happened?" Darcie asked.

"I killed him," Candy said. "Good riddance."

"Is that what you do, kill people?" Darcie said.

"You think I would be dumb enough to answer that," she said.

I heard footsteps and raised the gun, pointed it at the door.

"Nobody else here," DeMax said as he ran in.

"I'll call the FBI," Darcie said. "Mecana, you call Verves. He should know too."

"Yeah, I will. DeMax, lay that AK down. We did all the shooting, you got me?"

"I got you." He wiped the stock with his shirt, laid it on the floor and sat down beside Darcie and Candy.

Darcie patted him on the shoulder. "Thanks, partner. You were great," she said and dialed her phone.

"You too," he said.

"The FBI is on their way," Darcie said a few minutes later. "I told them to call before they drove in so we wouldn't shoot them. They said they would be here in less than an hour."

"I had to leave a message for Verves," I said. "Told him to call the FBI, too."

DeMax and I sat down with our eyes on Candy.

Something about Fritz was still bothering me but I couldn't put my finger on it. I stared at him lying on his back. The four bullet holes were in a tight grouping that tore a hole in his heart, all in one place.

The light bulb turned on.

That's what was bothering me. It was the same number of bullets and the same pattern as Kane.

About forty minutes later, I was making sure Candy stayed in one place.

Darcie's phone rang. "They're coming in," she said.

"I'll go outside and greet them," I said.

"I'll give you a million dollars to let me go," Candy said.

"Thought you weren't going to give us anymore money," I said.

"For the right reasons I will," she said. "Just say I got away."

"Can't do that. My daddy would turn over in his grave," I said.

"You're a simpleton, Mecana," Candy said.

"Maybe so. We misjudged you," I said. "You set Fillmore up as a scapegoat, murdered your husband, double-crossed Fritz and were using us to eliminate your adversaries."

"Because I'm smarter than you," Candy said.

"Not anymore."

CHAPTER 14

I heard a car drive up to the gate and walked outside with an AK-47 and stood in the shadows by the door. A black Mercedes like the one Fritz had been driving pulled up and a man leaned out the driver's-side window and shot the lock off the gate.

Hope that's the FBI, I thought.

He saw me and yelled, "FBI coming in."

"Come on," I yelled. "We're expecting you."

They drove through the gate with a SWAT van behind and stopped inside, behind my truck. The back door of the van swung open and ten men ran out, fully combat dressed, three taking positions on me. The others ran past me into the building.

I stepped out of the shadow. "I'm Thomas Mecana. I'm the one who called you." I showed the rifle over my head and slowly sat it down.

The man driving the Mercedes got out and walked up to me holding a Glock. He seemed to be the one in charge. He was tall and fit-looking with trimmed wavy black hair and wearing the traditional FBI attire: white shirt, black suit and tie, with a careful walk.

The one in the passenger side opened his door and stood behind it; looking at me, his bald head shining.

The tall one kicked the AK-47 away and said, "Turn around and lean against the wall," and patted me down. "Let's see some ID. Move slow."

I carefully removed my wallet and showed him my driver's license and PI card.

"Everybody in there friendlies?" he asked.

"The live ones are," I said. "Except for maybe Candy Kane."

He stuck his Glock back in his coat. We shook hands and went inside, the others following our lead.

Two were in the room with the dead guys and the others were in the room with my people and the dead Fritz.

"I'm Special Agent Bradford," he said and looked at Candy Kane. "Mrs. Kane, you'll have to come with us, the CIA wants you."

"Are you arresting me?" Candy asked.

"Yes, for the CIA."

"And do you have a warrant?" Darcie said. "I'm an attorney. We don't want her to walk."

"We picked one up from Judge Davis before we got here. Here's the one for her." He handed it to Darcie. She read the warrant and looked at Candy.

"The cops want you now," Darcie said.

The bald-headed man walked up to Agent Bradford. "I'm Agent Franks," he said, looking at us. "The crime scene and coroner squads are on the way. I've made a security check on everyone, and Mrs. Kane, you are only one we will have to hold. Unless we find causes here to change that."

A few seconds later, Chief Verves poked his head in the door, hesitated for a moment and walked in. "Bodies up to your ass again, Mecana," he said.

"All necessary, Chief," I said. "Agent Bradford, this is Chief Verves of Homicide in Dallas."

"Know of you, Chief," Bradford said, shaking hands. "He's right, these were some bad dudes with murder in mind."

"I heard," Verves said. "I see you have Mrs. Kane?"

"We have a warrant for her arrest," Bradford said.

"We have some more questions for her when we can," Verves said.

"Probably be a while; we've got priority on her," Bradford said. "Franks and I will take her in tonight."

"Looks like you're not going to need us now," Verves said. "Mecana, we need to talk when you get through here."

"Sure, Chief," I said.

"They can go," Bradford said.

We walked out behind Verves and stopped him on the veranda.

"Chief, we need a ride downtown," I said. "They threw my keys away. You can drop us off at the rental agency so we can pick up Darcie's car. They're open all night. We can talk about Candy on the way."

"Get in," he said.

We loaded up with Sergeant Edward Maddox at the wheel, a twenty-year police veteran. Mattox backed out and we got back on the freeway.

"Mecana," Verves said. "Mrs. Kane has a carrying permit for a 9mm pistol. She said someone stole it when I called her yesterday. The only place we can think of that we haven't looked is her car, it's disappeared. She said you have the keys and she doesn't know where it is."

"I have the keys but I couldn't find the car, either," I said.

"If the gun checks out, she probably did it," Verves said.

"She killed Fritz during our fight with his own gun. Four tight shots to the heart, same as Kane. That was no accident. That was shooting."

"Talk to the FBI Chief, you don't know the half of it. It's unbelievable," Darcie said.

"Learned a lot in the last few hours," Verves said. "The FBI and CIA are investigating Kane, Fritz and Mrs. Kane together. They found more associates that were involved with them in some sort of terrorist group."

Verves phone rang and he answered it.

"My god," he said. "We're on the way." He turned to his driver, "Head for 4th and Berryville, Maddox."

"Got it." Maddox wheeled around, turned the siren on and flew down the street, headed for Berryville.

"Mrs. Kane escaped in her car with some young man who shot the agents," Verves said.

Ten minutes later we could see flashing lights across the street at an intersection. Cruisers and ambulances were blocking the street both ways at 4th and Berryville. We weaved our way through and stopped next to an FBI Mercedes with all four doors open.

They had Agent Bradford on a gurney, carrying him to an ambulance, and Franks lying on a stretcher on the sidewalk with a blanket over his head.

Maddox cut everything off and we jumped out and ran to Agent Bradford.

"What happened," Verves said, looking at Bradford. "You get hit?"

"Shoulder," Bradford said.

"Can you talk?" Verves said.

"Yes. A young man rammed us at a stoplight and shot Franks in the head. I ducked but he shot me in the shoulder and grabbed Mrs. Kane out of the car. She called him Cactus, I think. I saw the tag number when they sped off. It was her car. They headed west on Berryville."

"She called him Cactus?" Verves said.

"Yes. Pretty sure," Bradford said and grimaced as they hit a crack in the concrete with the gurney.

"What did he look like?" Verves said.

"That's the pilot who worked for Kane," I said.

"Stay out of this, Mecana," Verves said and turned back to Bradford. "What did he look like?"

"Maybe in his twenties, about six feet, muscular," Bradford said. "Black hair and dark eyes. Carrying what looked like a 9mm."

"Okay, guys, get him in the ambulance," Verves said as two medics wheeled the agent away. "That must have been her gun."

"Fillmore is right, she's a devil of a woman," I said. "She's headed to France and that may have been her lover Cactus who shot them. And he's going to fly her to France in Kane's private jet."

"Why haven't you told me this before," Verves said.

"We just found out a few hours ago," I said.

"Stay here, you're not going to the airport," Verves said.

"We've got to go, chief," I said. "This is our ass, too."

"Well, shit. Head to DFW, Maddox," Verves said. "If they're going to France then that's probably where they're going to leave."

We all piled in, slammed the doors and headed to the airport.

"Maddox, open up the net and put out what we know," Verves said.

"I got it," Maddox said, "opening things up right now."

He punched in Candy's boyfriend's alias 'Cactus.' The descriptions and plate numbers matched.

Less than five minutes later, a call from a cruiser came back saying the car had been spotted on Mockingbird Lane. They were going to Love Field.

Another call came in saying they turned on a side street and cut through a fence outside Love Field, jumped out of the car and ran to Gate 15 to a Lear jet sitting outside a hanger.

"They'll have to cut them off on the runway," Darcie said.

More than thirty police cars had arrived, along with SWAT teams at the fence, and directed their lights at the jet to blind them; but it didn't seem to slow them down. The jet made its way out on the runway, spun around and revved up the engines.

"Now we know how she got to New York and back in one night," I said.

"Make sure the control tower doesn't give them permission to take off," Verves said, while Maddox put out the word.

A SWAT trooper ran up to the gate, pulled a rocket launcher off his back, and readied it for firing.

"Are they going after the cockpit or the engines," I said.

"Doesn't matter at this point," Verves said.

"It does if we want to find out the whole story."

"Damn, Mecana. You always want the whole enchilada, this may be it."

"No, there's a lot more," I said.

Just as the trooper fired, the jet turned and the rocket cruised by, missing and blowing up a fence on the other side of the runway.

The jet took off down the runway. It picked up speed, lifted off at the end of the runway, banked to the right and began climbing.

Four or five seconds later, an explosion like a war zone blast blew the engines completely off the wings. Two big burning boxes shot out the side of the aircraft; money spilling out, floating and twisting and turning as it fell to the ground, a few bills catching fire on the way down through burning pieces of the aircraft.

The jet was burned to a crisp by the time it hit the ground, long before a firetruck was in sight. Later, no human remains would be found. At least none large enough to recognize.

Spectators started running out on the runway grabbing money.

Police cars drove out on the runway, chasing everyone off and picking up the money and stuffing it in bags.

When several firetrucks arrived, there was nothing left to save. They joined the rest in picking up money.

"I'm goin' to get me some money," DeMax said, reaching for the door handle.

"You do and I'll arrest you," Verves said.

"What about all of them," DeMax said, pointing at the runway.

"They're gathering up the money for evidence," Verves said.

"Bullshit," DeMax said. "You ain't going to see any of that damn money again."

"Cool it, I'll get it back," Verves said. "The media's going to call this a terrorist attack and be all over it by morning."

"Kane, Fritz and Candy were dealing with terrorists," I said.

A report started coming in on the car's computer screen. It stated Cactus was the alias of a former convicted drug pilot. Born in Mexico, real name Jose Eduardo Gomez, 29 years-old. No flight plan filed to New York or to France.

"Bet you that was Fritz's doing," I said.

"Just be thankful the one's who you shot were in self-defense," Verves said.

"They all were. The game's over, we win. Drop us off at the Rental Right Car Company, Chief," I said. "I'll touch base with you tomorrow after I retrieve my truck."

"Okay," Verves said. "You hear him, Maddox?"

"Yeah," Maddox said.

A big glob of foul-smelling black smoke drifted overhead and disappeared into the night, leaving flames flickering from small scattered pieces of the airplane on the runway – Candy and Cactus on their way to hell.

CHAPTER 15

My bed at the house felt great and Darcie even better next to me. I sat up, slipped on my pants, left my Glock on the nightstand and walked into the other bedroom to check on DeMax; he was asleep. I went back in the living room and turned on the TV.

Every channel kept repeating the spectacular crash of the jet, raining money as it burned to the ground. There was very little about the participants involved and even less left to find.

After four or five minutes of television, Darcie and De-Max came in and sat down on the couch with me. We were amazed as the scenes kelp unfolding over and over.

"I ain't flying anymore," I said.

"Me either," Darcie said.

"I never did," DeMax said.

My phone rang, it was Verves.

"Morning, Chief," I said.

"I guess you've seen the crash on TV," Verves said.

"Yeah, like what we saw," I said.

"The FBI and CIA have arrested another ten people, including a terrorist by the name of Ali Juror Mohamed, who rigged the explosives on the jet for Landon Fritz."

"Figured that," I said. "Birds of a feather flock together. Fritz knew she would run with Cactus in Kane's jet."

"She had as much of Kane's money converted to cash as she could and put it on the plane," Verves said. "Maybe two or three billion. They found video that showed her closing the door to his room at 1:30 the morning he was murdered. And she may have murdered over a dozen around the world when she was hypnotized, according to info from the CIA. Personally, I think the hypnotizing thing is a lot of bullshit."

"Not necessarily," I said. "Doesn't matter now, though, unless she wasn't the only one."

"That's a horrible thought," Verves said. "Don't want to think about it anymore. Come in and give your statement today and go. They said they dropped all the charges against you three."

"The right thing to do," I said.

"What are you going to do now," Verves said.

"I have to go to Austin and give my daughters their graduation presents pretty soon."

"Think I'm going to retire," Verves said. "Wore down to a nub."

"And who's going to take care of me?"

"Simon Necessary will take over. He'll also be bringing my daughter Sunday with him from robbery to homicide."

"You and Simon go back a long ways, don't you," I said.

"We broke in together. All his kids are grown and married except for Angela; she has a gourmet restaurant for the rich."

"I heard about it but never been there," I said.

"Nice place," Verves said. "Sunday and Angela are good friends. We raised them together. Might be best to talk to Sunday if you need anything when I retire."

"Sunday's a good cop. I'll do that. Thanks for everything," I said.

"You bet. I'll let you know when I retire so you can buy me something," he said and was gone.

I laid the phone on the couch and watched Darcie and DeMax as they stared at the TV.

"You guys ready to make a statement to the cops so we can move on," I said. "I'm flabbergasted. Can't quite figure out how I feel about what happened to Candy."

"No words for it," Darcie said.

"I thought I had already seen the unbelievable and the impossible with Lisa," I said. "But Candy took it a step beyond. Her ashes are probably blowing in the wind somewhere."

"Yeah, too weird for me," DeMax said. "Won't ever let anyone hypnotize me."

"You going to Austin with me, Darcie?" I said.

"No, I'm going house hunting," she said.

"House hunting? Are you moving out?" I said.

"No, I want us to move out of this house and into our house."

"Ours?"

"Yeah and plan a wedding," she said and smiled.

"Really?" I said.

"When you get back from Austin," she said.

"Let me get this straight. You don't care if I spend money on the kids, and we're going to get married when I get back from Austin?"

"That's right, if you still want me," Darcie said.

I jumped up, whisked her off the couch and rolled around with her on the floor, groping and kissing her passionately.

"Stop, you're embarrassing me in front of DeMax," Darcie said.

"Don't bother me," DeMax said. "Seen a lot more than that."

"You want to go to Austin with me and be my best man DeMax?" I said.

"You want me to kick that boyfriend's ass?" DeMax said and grinned.

"Only if he wants to drive Emily's new car."

"He will," Darcie said.

"Maybe I was wrong. Somebody up there does like me."

THE END

THE END

About the Author

John L. Lansdale was born and raised in East Texas. He is married to the love of his life Mary. They have four children. He is a retired Army reserve Psychological Operations Officer and a combat veteran with numerous medals and awards. Past roles include inventor, country music songwriter and performer, and television programmer. He produced and directed the Television Special "Ladies of Country Music." He has also produced several albums in Nashville, hosted his own radio shows and won awards for producing and writing radio and television commercials. He was a writer and editor of a business newspaper. He has worked as a comic book writer for Tales from the Crypt, IDW, Grave Tales, Cemetery Dance and several more. He co-authored the Shadows West and Hell's Bounty novels with his brother Joe R. Lansdale. He is also the author of Horse of a Different Color, Slow Bullet, Zombie Gold, When the Night Bird Sings, Broken Moon, Long Walk Home, The Last Good Day and several other titles.

THE MECANA SERIES by John L. Lansdale
#1 - Horse of a Different Color
#2 - When the Night Bird Sings
#3 - Twisted Justice

Titles by John L. Lansdale
Slow Bullet
Long Walk Home
Zombie Gold
The Last Good Day
Broken Moon
Shadows West (with Joe R. Lansdale)
Hell's Bounty (with Joe R. Lansdale)
Boy and Hog (Short Story)
Boy and Hog Return (Short Story)
Emergency Christmas (Short Story)
Tales from the Crypt (Comic Series)
That Hellbound Train (Graphic Novel)
Yours Truly, Jack the Ripper (Graphic Novel)
Shadow Warrior (Graphic Novel)
Justin Case (Graphic Novel)

SLOW BULLET
by John L. Lansdale
Now available from BookVoice Publishing

A "page-turner... Those who like their thrillers with a heavy dose of violent action will be satisfied." - *Publishers Weekly*

In this timely novel, Clark McKay, a retired Army Special Forces Colonel, has developed a drinking problem after losing his wife and son in a car accident, as well as from the nightmares of his Vietnam days. And he's not getting any younger. In spite of his problems, he is determined to find out who murdered his best friend and his friend's wife.

A Washington D.C. detective refuses to believe McKay has found the murderer, a former CIA operative and arms dealer who murdered McKay's friend because he discovered the truth behind the assassination of JFK – preventing President John F. Kennedy from ending the Vietnam War.

McKay learns there are CIA documents his friend hid that will prove the conspiracy to be true. His search for these documents takes him all over the world. On his journey, after wading through corruption, McKay is brought to the conclusion that he may have to resort to murder if justice is to be served.

What happened over fifty years ago is still with us today. In fact, many still doubt the "lone gunman" theory put forth by the Warren Commission. Could there truly have been a conspiracy to keep JFK from ending the war?

Truth and fiction make an interesting mixture in this fast-paced and entertaining novel. There are always those who escape justice. One hand washes the other, unless you have someone like Clark McKay who is willing to pay the ultimate price.

"*Slow Bullet* is a straight-ahead thriller...it's about action, and there's plenty of that. Check it out."
– *Bill Crider's Pop Culture Magazine*

HORSE OF A DIFFERENT COLOR
a Mecana Novel
by John L. Lansdale
Now available from BookVoice Publishing

Someone is murdering and mutilating young women in a Dallas suburb, using the same techniques as a case down in Houston the previous year.

When the second body is found, it seems the killer has moved his hunting grounds to the Dallas area.

As the body count rises, Detective Thomas Mecana – a divorced fifteen-year veteran of the Dallas Police Department – is assigned to the case.

He prides himself on always getting his man, but his tried-and-true methods of the past are not working.

To make matters worse, his supervisor assigns him a new partner, a young officer who has never before worked a murder case.

Add in two teenage daughters creating problems at home, and a boss threatening to fire him at work, and Mecana's life begins to unravel as he hones in on his suspect.

With hard work, and some luck, Mecana and his partner discover a most-unusual serial killer case with murder in its very genes.

They discover some evidence is so strange and unbelievable, it might be best left alone.

Checkmate.

"...the author's innate ability to spin a complex tale painted with vivid characters and intense suspense provides readers with a well-paced book that they may find difficult to set down." – Ricky L. Brown, *Amazing Stories*

LONG WALK HOME
a novel by
John L. Lansdale

Ten-year-old Trenton O'Rourke's life was changed forever during the summer of 1944. He and his family lived on a fading farm like many others in the small town of Angel Point, Mississippi. With family members fighting in World War II overseas, and rising racial tensions back home, what was normally a routine summer turned into a nightmare of murder, loss, trying to cope with hard times to survive and surprise learning experiences of growing up. Trenton's life would have never been what it was had it not been for a chance encounter with someone nobody expected.

BookVoice Pocket Stories
Short Stories by John L. Lansdale

BOY AND HOG

In the deep woods, anything can happen.
A group of white-collar workers with a hand-drawn map
trek into the wilderness for a hunting expedition.
But out there, will they be the hunters or the prey?

BOY AND HOG RETURN

While on patrol, two game wardens stumble onto a grisly
scene hidden deep in the woods. With backup on the way,
will the wardens survive the wait, or will unexpected visitors send them to an early grave?

EMERGENCY CHRISTMAS

Tells the story of the Albright family at Christmastime, and
the guest who surprises them just in time for the holiday.
Along the way, the Albrights discover sometimes crisis
brings a family closer together.

Keep your eyes peeled for

THE LAST GOOD DAY
by John L. Lansdale

and

BROKEN MOON
by John L. Lansdale

Two new Westerns from
John L. Lansdale and BookVoice Publishing

STAY CONNECTED
WITH BOOKVOICE
AND
JOHN L. LANSDALE

Follow us online at
www.bvpstore.com
www.bookvoicepublishing.com
www.twitter.com/mybookvoice
www.goodreads.com/johnllansdale
www.facebook.com/bookvoicepublishing

www.ingramcontent.com/pod-product-compliance
Lightning Source LLC
Chambersburg PA
CBHW020620120726
47905CB00003B/879